ID0407753

A Perfect
Universe

A Perfect Universe

Ten Stories

Scott O'Connor

SCOUT PRESS

New York   London   Toronto   Sydney   New Delhi

Scout Press
An Imprint of Simon & Schuster, Inc.
1230 Avenue of the Americas
New York, NY 10020

First Scout Press hardcover edition February 2018

SCOUT PRESS and colophon are trademarks of Simon and Schuster.

For information about special discounts for bulk purchases, please contact Simon & Schuster Special Sales at 1-866-506-1949 or business@simonandschuster.com.

The Simon & Schuster Speakers Bureau can bring authors to your live event. For more information or to book an event, contact the Simon & Schuster Speakers Bureau at 1-866-248-3049 or visit our website at www.simonspeakers.com.

Interior design by Jaime Putorti

Manufactured in the United States of America

10 9 8 7 6 5 4 3 2 1

Library of Congress Cataloging-in-Publication Data
Names: O'Connor, Scott, author.
Title: A Perfect Universe / Scott O'Connor.
Description: First Scout Press hardcover edition. | New York : Scout Press, 2018.
Identifiers: LCCN 2017014957 (print) | LCCN 2017021407 (ebook) | ISBN 9781507204061 (ebook) | ISBN 150720406X (ebook) | ISBN 9781507204054 (hardback) | ISBN 1507204051 (hardcover)
Subjects: | BISAC: FICTION / Short Stories (single author). | FICTION / Literary. | FICTION / General.
Classification: LCC PS3615.C595 (ebook) | LCC PS3615.C595 A6 2017 (print) | DDC 813/.6—dc23
LC record available at https://lccn.loc.gov/2017014957

ISBN 978-1-5072-0405-4
ISBN 978-1-5072-0406-1 (ebook)

Some of the stories from *A Perfect Universe* were originally published as follows: "Hold On" and "Jane's Wife" in *ZYZZYVA*; "It Was Over So Quickly, Doug" in *The Rattling Wall*; "Golden State" as an Amazon Kindle Single; "Interstellar Space" in *F(r)iction* and *Six Shorts 2015: The Finalists for the Sunday Times EFG Short Story Award*; "In the Red" in *VLAK*; "Hold On" was listed as Distinguished in *The Best American Short Stories 2015*; "Interstellar Space" was shortlisted for the Sunday Times EFG Short Story Award.

For Oscar, who tells the best stories

in sci-fi they call it a starship
and those aboard the seed of mankind
the lone traveler could be any soul
mind adrift in time, mind adrift/the body
turned outward imagines a perfect universe
distant matter the cosmic rumble in
fire and gas, the spinnings of stars,
the flight of ghosts
galaxies on the fly, heaven's flame, spheres
whirring by
the sky spilling over its edges, heart
sparking a violent wonder

—Wanda Coleman, *I Want to Grow Old Like That*

Contents

Hold On

The first thing I remember is the woman's voice, amplified through the megaphone, calling my name. *Castillo, Robert.* I opened my eyes, but only knew they were open because I could feel my lids moving. There was no change in the darkness.

Cuarón, Eduardo. Daniels, Margaret. Daniels, Rachel. I couldn't move. Everything hurt. There was no light, not much air. But the names kept coming. *Diaz, Rosalie. Eaglesham, Jessica. Faye, Renee.* I started screaming, *Help me, I'm under here!*, but my voice went nowhere, it just died in the debris around my face. *Hernandez, Adrian. Hull, Leticia.* I screamed until I realized how stupid it was, using all the precious air. When I was finally quiet, I could hear her again.

Hold on, she said. *We're coming for you.*

The names continued. But after every ten or so, she'd stop and say, *Hold on, we're coming,* or *Don't give up, we're digging.*

And they were. Once I stopped screaming, I could hear that, too. The sound of shovels and picks ringing in the rubble.

There were 146 names after mine, and when she got to the end of the list, she started again at the beginning.

There are about 5,600 pay phones left within the Los Angeles city limits. There are nine on the Santa Monica Pier, eighteen in and around the Convention Center downtown. The Vons supermarket in Echo Park has six. Dodger Stadium has eight, one of which is consistently in need of repair.

My department at the phone company was responsible for these units. We cleaned and serviced, collected the change from the coin boxes, and, as of the last few years, demolished a handful of underachievers every month, casualties of cellular progress.

Their destruction was my least favorite part of the job. It felt like a kind of forced euthanasia. Eva always got upset when I made that comparison. She thought it was disrespectful to the elderly. But some of those phones were as old as senior citizens. They had put in a lifetime of service, day and night, weekends, holidays. Some of those phones had never failed until their lines were snipped and they were ripped from their sockets and tossed into the back of one of our trucks.

I always tried to leave them with their dignity. On that one day a month of grim-reaper duty, I'd clear away the cigarette butts and scrape off the hardened bubble gum, spray the faceplate and receiver with disinfectant one last time, and then, gently but firmly, cut the line.

* * *

"Are we losing our pay phone?"

"You are. I'm sorry."

"Well, I can't—I guess nobody really used it."

"Two hundred dollars a month."

"Excuse me?"

"It averaged about two hundred dollars a month. That's four hundred calls."

"Really? I never saw a single . . .Then why are you taking it down?"

"Two hundred dollars barely pays for the dial tone. This unit used to do close to a thousand, and that was when it was a quarter a call."

"Well, I'm sorry to see it go for some reason. Out with the old, in with the— Did you feel that?"

"Feel what?"

"That. Whoa. Did you feel that?"

I don't know how many times I've tried to describe it to reporters and friends and strangers who stop me on the street. *What's it like?*

For a while I just said that it was like being buried alive, which is true, and also, I thought, sort of funny. I hoped it would lighten the mood a little. People didn't want light. They'd nod and look deep into my eye. *I can't imagine,* they'd say. Women took my arm. Men set their hands on my shoulders. As if touching me would give them some kind of understanding. As if this were something I could pass on, something I could share.

What's it like? the network newsmagazine reporter asked me, leaning forward in her chair. *What's. It. Like.*

There was movement back in the darkness of the studio, a camera swiveling from the reporter's face to mine. On one of the monitors I could see the shot: a slow zoom in, a close-up on my eyepatch. I could feel everyone in the studio—the reporter, the cameramen, the producers back in the booth—waiting for the answer. *Twenty-five million,* someone had said during the last commercial break. Estimated viewers, leaning toward their TVs.

What's it like?

"I can't describe it," I said, letting myself off the hook, letting twenty-five million people down. "It's indescribable."

By the time the woman with the megaphone had gotten to *Miller, Jessica,* I'd started to calm down. I was on the list. They knew I was there. A few minutes before I'd walked into the building, I'd answered a call from my supervisor at the phone company, so he'd known I was inside when it came down.

I lay there and waited. Whenever people talk about how brave I was, how heroic, I always want to say, *I just lay there.* Everyone else did all the work. But no one wants to hear that. They need to believe there was some great inner strength tapped, some proof of the resilience of the human spirit in its darkest hour.

But there wasn't. I just lay there.

* * *

I was in the hospital for six weeks. I went through fourteen surgeries. I lost an eye, I gained a walking cane, though the doctors said I was young enough that the limp probably wouldn't be so pronounced in a few years. I'm told that I displayed a tremendous amount of bravery in the way I handled this, too, but I don't see it. What was I going to do, throw myself out the window? I was too doped up to get out of bed.

I spent most of the time in the hospital watching the news. They were still showing footage of the rescue: the cops and firefighters pulling me out, carrying the stretcher down the mountain of steel and cement; the huge work lights holding back the darkness; the workers and newspeople cheering and crying. That shot where, right before they load me into the ambulance, I raise my hand. I don't know what I was doing. Feeling for my eye, probably. That same shot, over and over. Raising my hand. Everybody cheers. The triumph of the will.

They showed earlier scenes, too. The first shots of the collapsed building. The swarm of sirens and flashing lights. The rescue workers digging day and night. The mayor telling the cameras, *This is no longer a rescue operation; this is a recovery operation.*

Every so often there was a shot where you could see the woman with the megaphone, pacing at the foot of the rubble. You could hear her under the voiceovers of the newscasters and guest experts. It's a wide shot, to get the full scope of the devastation, and she's tiny in the frame. A black woman, middle-aged, heavy-set, with a bit of a southern drawl. You can hear it softening the corners of the names she's saying. *Pollack, Henry. Pullman, Sarah.* Her back is to the camera. She never stops talking, never lowers the megaphone.

Hold on, she says. *We're coming for you.*

What's it like?

It's like something so ordinary that it didn't seem worth mentioning. Like the real answer would be more of a letdown than saying it was indescribable.

What's it like? It's like when my brother and I used to wrestle on the living room floor. He was twice as big, and inevitably he'd pin me on my back. And for a few seconds, there was something exciting about feeling completely powerless, being at someone else's mercy. But then he wouldn't let me up, and the more I struggled the tighter he held me down. It was the most awful feeling.

That's what it was like. It felt like that.

For three days.

Just before they released me from the hospital, I broke up with Eva. I told her that I needed some time, some space. I needed to get my head around what had happened. I could tell she was trying to keep her emotions in check, which must have been some struggle for her. Remaining calm, supportive, understanding. Nodding at me like I was a kid or a pet. As if this was a predictable stage of whatever psychological process I was going through. She'd talked to the hospital shrink, too. She was following best-practice protocol. No scene, no tears. A muffled end to our two years together.

Before she left the hospital room, she took my hand. "Call me," she said. "Whenever you're ready to talk."

I got asked a lot about working at the phone company. What I did there, how I'd liked the job. Suddenly all this interest. I didn't know how to answer. It was what I did. It was just my job.

What I really cared about was playing bass in the band. Heading down to Dido's garage after work and running through eight or nine songs and a case of beer and Dido's mom bringing out plates of beans and rice drizzled with tomatillo that blew our ears out way more than anything we were playing. That was what got me through the workday, the thought of that. That and Eva. But when people asked, I couldn't really mention Eva anymore and I wasn't returning Dido's calls. *Hey, bro, I was thinking we should get the band back* and I'd skip to the next message. For the longest time the band was one of the only things I cared about, and now I couldn't even stand to listen to Dido's voice.

I tried not to worry about it. The shrink had said this would happen. Disassociation from formerly cherished persons and activities. He said it would be temporary. He said the medication would help.

I got a copy of the footage. I called one of the local TV stations and explained who I was and asked if I could have a DVD.

"Are you writing a book?" the producer asked.

"Yeah," I said. "I'm writing a book."

They sent eighteen discs. Seventy-two hours of footage. I watched it all, never fast-forwarding. I wanted to experience it like everyone else had experienced it. By then I was a pro at staying in one place for long periods of time.

I sat on my couch and gasped and shook when the first pictures of the scene started coming in, the confusion over what was happening and then the sickening realization. That collective intake of breath that must have occurred across the country. *Oh my God.*

The rescuers arrived. The digging began. A media area was constructed outside the main entrance to the hospital, a podium with the city seal and a black bouquet of microphones. A guy from the office of the mayor was there every hour or so, giving a briefing. The fire chief, the chief of police. Every once in a while they'd try to talk to a rescue worker, but the workers waved them off. They were too busy digging.

Cynthia Lopez from the local news was the narrator for most of the footage, recapping what was known, breaking in with new developments. One day, two days. Most of the new developments updated the body count, the names of the deceased. Then the mayor was at the podium. *This is no longer a rescue operation; this is a recovery operation.* The bulldozers, the dump trucks. The firefighters standing in front of the machines, refusing to give up, holding their shovels like swords, keeping the trucks at bay.

But throughout the footage, the woman with the megaphone was always there, in the background, the periphery of shots. Her

back to the camera, pacing, calling our names. I yelled at the TV
for her to turn around. *Rawlings, Catherine. Rolston, Barney.*

Turn around! Turn around!

She never turned around.

"Do you have any words for the firefighters, for the rescue workers?"

"Thank you."

"Is there something you want to say to them, to the men and
women who didn't give up?"

"Thank you."

On disc fifteen, there's a clip of me leaving the hospital,
wheeled through the front doors by one of my surgeons and an
army of nurses and administrators and orderlies. The reporters
follow with mics and cameras as I'm pushed toward the ambulance that would take me to the first rehab center.

I remember this clip. The other patients at the rehab center
watched it over and over in the TV room the first few days I was
there.

"—the workers who defied the orders of the mayor, and kept
digging through that last night?"

"Thank you."

"Do you have anything to say to the mayor, who threatened
to fire anyone who wouldn't get out of the way of the bulldozers?"

"Yes. I do. Fuck you, you prick. I was still alive under there."

Even with the bleeped curse, that line always got a lot of
applause in the TV room.

* * *

One of the cops told me to stop by the First Street station anytime I wanted. *Our house is your house,* he'd said. I'd gone a couple of times early on, because I was having trouble sleeping and the police station was the only place open at 3 A.M. We drank coffee and they told stories about the days of the dig. But after a while I stopped going. I didn't belong there. They had done something heroic. I was just a guy who'd been in the wrong place at the wrong time.

I went back after I watched the DVDs. I had gone to an electronics place downtown and bought a machine that hooks up to your DVD player and prints out still frames from the video. I printed a handful of the best frames of the woman with the megaphone, the ones where you could make out what she was wearing, where you could almost see her face. I took them down to the station and showed the cops.

They remembered her, but didn't know who she was. Everyone thought she was a city official of some sort. She had the list of the missing; she had a megaphone. They couldn't remember her *not* being there, even after the mayor told everyone to abandon ship. It wasn't until they'd pulled me free, after the ambulances had left and things started to clear out, that anyone noticed she was gone.

I had, actually, received a lot of money for the book rights to my story. The ghostwriter is a woman about my age, a columnist for a weekly newspaper down in San Diego. She's smart and pretty, and six months ago, before the cane and the eyepatch, I probably would have fallen all over myself trying to impress her.

We meet at a coffee shop in my neighborhood every morning and I tell her my life story, up to and including the day I took the elevator to the twenty-sixth floor to pull that pay phone, and then the three days after. She asks me what the worst part of the ordeal was. I tell her that it sounds stupid, but that the worst part was not sleeping. I was so tired, but I was afraid that if I fell asleep I'd miss the rescue workers getting close and if I didn't call out, they'd pass me by. So I stayed awake.

She asks me what it felt like when the firefighters digging nearby finally heard me, when they took my hand and held it while others dug furiously to get me free. What I remembered most.

What I remembered most was the sound of the woman's voice through the megaphone, getting clearer and louder as the debris was pulled away.

Hold on, baby. We're getting you out. I told you, baby. I told you.

"What did you say?" the ghostwriter asks. "You said something on the stretcher, on the way out. It's hard to hear on any of the tapes."

"I was delirious," I tell her. "I don't know what I said."

She writes this down, then crosses it out. "We'll think of something later."

It sounded like she knew us, the woman with the megaphone. She gave each of our names a distinct personality, like she was reading off a list of friends. Every once in a while I heard what sounded like another voice and the woman with the megaphone would yell, *Hold on,* and I wanted to yell, too. *Margaret Daniels, hold on! Adrian Hernandez, hold on!* When I imagined our rescue, I pictured us all standing by the rubble, shaking, dazed, blankets on our shoulders, paper coffee cups in our hands. I imagined friends for life. Something more than friends, even, sharing something only we could understand. *My husband doesn't get it,* Leticia Hull would tell me, weeks later, years later. *But you get it.*

I imagined all sorts of silly shit. Michael Gordon and Henry Pollack—guys I'd never met, guys I'd never even seen, but who I could still see clearly—with me at a Dodgers game, at a sports bar, at a show, not saying a goddamned thing about it. Not needing to. Just knowing.

In the hospital, Eva had said, *You survived. You made it, you were the only one.* And I know it makes no sense, but I couldn't help but hate her for taking them all away.

Dido kept calling. We hadn't rehearsed in months, hadn't played a show in almost a year, but offers were coming in for gigs and radio appearances, a couple of TV spots. There was some record company attention. All of this was based on what had happened to me rather than any genuine interest in the band, but the guys didn't seem to care. An opportunity was an opportunity.

We called a rehearsal in Dido's garage, just like the old days, and everyone drank and smoked and wailed away, but I kept jumping every time Dido crashed the cymbals, to the point where

I was literally freaking out after an overly long drum fill and had to leave the garage to catch my breath.

Dido followed me, pissed. I was blowing our chance. We shouted back and forth while the other guys hung in the doorway and smoked and made half-assed attempts to intervene. A couple of the neighbors stopped watering the scrub brush in their front yards to watch. It was a real scene. You fucking this, you fucking that. You've always, you've never, blah blah blah. Dido started to run out of gas. I don't think he expected me to push back so hard. I've never been much of a fighter, but it felt good to yell, so I shouted until I was the only one shouting. I didn't care who heard—the neighbors, Dido's mom back in the house. I just kept screaming at him that I couldn't take the noise anymore, throwing up my hands and limping back to my car and shouting that we were a shitty band, we'd always been a shitty band, and three days pinned under the concrete hadn't changed that.

I believed you. That's what I said on the stretcher, on the way out of the pile. The last thing the woman had said through the megaphone, right before they got me to the ambulance, was *I told you we were coming, baby.* And I didn't know if she could hear me or not, but I said, *I believed you.*

I still have trouble sleeping. I lie in bed for a few hours and then get up and walk the hills above my apartment, over around the reservoir. I come back dragging, out of breath, legs aching, but still not exhausted enough to sleep, or at least to sleep in the way I want to, without those dreams of Dodgers games and bars and concerts, Leticia Hull telling me that I'm the only one who understands.

A couple of the First Street cops came by my apartment. One black, one white. They were in civilian clothes and I couldn't remember their names. I've been having trouble with names. We stood in the living room. I offered to make some coffee, but they passed.

The black cop said there'd been a complaint. Apparently I've been calling Eva in the middle of the night, and when she answers I scream into the phone. I don't say anything, I just scream. When she stopped picking up, I started screaming into her voice mail.

He played me the recordings. It sure sounded like my voice. After a minute or so, he turned it off. The white cop stood by the door and looked at his shoes.

The black cop said that they'd talked her out of filing a restraining order, convinced her not to speak to the news. I thanked him and told him that it wouldn't happen again. I'd been having trouble sleeping, I said, but my doctor prescribed something and it wouldn't be a problem anymore.

"Are you sure you're okay?" he asked. I was embarrassed that he had to deal with this, with me.

"I'm fine," I said. "Every day I wake up and think how lucky I am to be alive."

The kindness of strangers has been overwhelming. The firefighters and police and rescue workers took up a collection to pay my medical bills, but the hospital waived them anyway. People from all over the world sent cards and letters, CDs and books. I received over a hundred Bibles. A car dealer in St. Louis sent me a brand-new Cadillac.

After I got out of the hospital, I tried to go back to work, but the phone company promoted me to an office job and I had trouble sitting still. I've had other opportunities, offers to do ads for everything from survival-themed workout videos to a line of fashion eyepatches, but I turned them all down. I look at the interviews with the ghostwriter as my real job now. So when she says that I look tired, that we can take a break for a few days if I'm not feeling up to it, I tell her that I'm fine, that I need to do this. It's good therapy.

I wonder what she knows. If she's talked to the police, or to Eva. She does a lot of research. Sometimes she brings up things about my life that I've forgotten.

I ask her about the woman with the megaphone. She says that she hasn't identified her yet. She wasn't sure that the woman was important to the story. I tell her that I was just curious, because she keeps showing up on the footage.

"We can ask one of the TV reporters," she says. "They might have gotten her name."

The whirlpool's the best part of rehab. The stretching and weight training are brutal, but I like to sit in the big plastic tub and close my eye, stretch out my arms and legs and sink into the heat.

I heave out a lungful of water and my trainer pulls his face from mine and rolls me onto my side. I heave some more and he pounds me on the back. My chest hurts from where he's been pushing on it. I open my eye. There's a circle of other trainers and patients standing over us.

"Can you breathe?" my trainer asks.

I nod, but can't stop coughing long enough to speak.

"You must have slipped and gone under," he says.

I nod, coughing, finally clearing my lungs. "Thank you," I say. "I must have slipped."

Cynthia Lopez meets me in the lobby of the TV studio. When we enter the newsroom, all of the reporters and newscasters are standing in the aisles between their desks, waiting for something. I'm afraid that it might be a birthday or retirement party, and I start to apologize for interrupting, but then they all applaud. For me.

She leads me through the crowd. One of the reporters has a copy of the newspaper where I was on the front page, lying on the stretcher, surrounded by firefighters and rescue workers, holding my arm up. The headline says, *Sole Survivor*. The reporter asks me to autograph it for his daughter.

We get to Cynthia Lopez's desk and she opens a spreadsheet on her computer. "I didn't know who she was. I assumed she was a city official. She had the list of the missing. She had a megaphone." She finds the entry and clicks the mouse. An interview transcription comes up on the screen.

"We only spoke for a second," Cynthia Lopez says. "She said she had to get back to work. Her name is Margaret Hamilton."

Cynthia Lopez reads to me from the screen, as if without my eye I've somehow lost that ability, too.

CL: Is that a current list of the missing?

MH: Unless they've pulled somebody out that I don't know about.

CL: Are you with the mayor's office? Is that where I can get an updated list?

MH: I'm not with the mayor.

CL: Are you from the hospital?

MH: I work at the post office on Vine and Selma in Hollywood.

CL: I'm sorry, then, I don't—

MH: I saw it on TV and came down.

CL: Came down why?

MH: Because there are people in there, honey. There are still people in there.

Hamilton, Margaret Anne. Widow of George, mother of Linda and Davis, grandmother of Craig and Tamara and George III. Born forty-six years ago in the same hospital I was taken to. Employee of the United States Postal Service for twenty-one years. Member of the Bethany Baptist Church on Eighth Street. Resident of the 2900 block of South St. Andrews Place.

I turn off the library computer. It's late afternoon. There are high school kids at all the other tables, sitting close together, huddled almost, ignoring their homework to look at me. The man with the eyepatch, the scars. Whispering, snickering. I stand and snarl, show my teeth. This is what they want. I move closer, dragging my leg. I lift the eyepatch.

The librarian asks me to leave, but I'm only giving them what they want.

The cops are back. This time it's the ghostwriter who's complaining about my calls. She's had to get her number changed.

The black cop puts his hand on my shoulder. It's not the same kind of touch I get from strangers asking, *What's it like?* It's a firm grip, a warning. It feels good. It makes me want to keep calling the ghostwriter, calling Eva, anyone, just so he'll come back.

"Stay off the phone," he says, turning to the door, and I feel like shouting at him, swinging at him, so he'll grab me again.

I couldn't sleep and so I walked the hills and around the reservoir and then farther into the city, ending up at her building just as the sun started to rise.

Her voice through the call box sounds just like her voice through the megaphone. Slightly over-amplified, metal-tinged, but deep and rich and warm. I have to stop myself from pressing the buzzer another time, just to hear it again.

She opens the door and recognizes me immediately.

"Oh my goodness," she says. "You look worse than when they pulled you out."

She looks older than I imagined. Uncoiled white strands stand up spring-like from the bun of her hair. There are gray puffs of skin under her eyes. Years of worry or lack of sleep. She's dressed in her postal uniform, getting ready for work.

"Can you help me?" I ask.

"Can I—"

She reaches up to my face. I close my eye and I can see her pacing on the news videos, her back to the camera. I close my eye and see nothing, just the darkness under the pile, waiting for her voice.

"Please," I say.

She's shaking, but her hand feels warm on my cheek. "Hold on, baby," she says. "You hear me? You hold on. We're going to get you out of there."

It Was Over So Quickly, Doug

So she's standing at the counter and she orders a tall half-caf. She's blonde, well-dressed. Business suit, nice shoes. She's got a phone bud in her ear and the cord down to the phone actually goes through her hoop earring, which means she put her jewelry on *around* the phone, got dressed *around* the phone, which probably tells you all you need to know. She's talking to her assistant or somebody on the other end of the call and ordering from me at the same time, and she's got this attitude, you know? Like I'm just some girl at the coffee shop who should just do whatever and not mind that she is so unbelievably rude for talking on the phone while she's ordering a cup of coffee from another real live human being.

It had already been that kind of morning, Doug. You remember. The markets were running off the fucking rails and I had a million messages from clients who all needed to be talked down from the ledge, so I really didn't need the hostility. I can't stand these coffee shop girls with chips on their shoulders because they're making five bucks an hour but they're still hipper than you. Than *thou*. It's like: get me my goddamn cup of coffee now, Nose Ring.

I'm already late, and the business lady was agitated, and the coffee chick had an attitude, and I'm checking the time and thinking, *Ladies, can't we all be pals and get this transaction done, because I've got a script meeting on the other side of the hill in half an hour.*

I go over to the urn, start to pour her coffee. And she says into her phone, "Hold on, Doug—holdonholdonholdon," like really fast, and then she says to me, "Waitasecond—let's make this something else, all right? I've changed my mind." I have to tell myself, *Jessie, do not spit in this woman's coffee.* I have to take an actual moment to stop myself. So I turn back to her, and raise my eyebrow, waiting, like, All right, what can I do for you now?

I just wanted something sweet, Doug. I didn't want regular coffee. It tears up my stomach. Even half-regular. I knew this was going to be a bitch of a day and I wanted something sweet, so I changed my mind.

So now the business lady is thinking and the coffee chick is glaring, and I just want to order, you know? Can we do without the drama? I've got somewhere to be.

She's staring at the menu up on the wall, twisting her mouth as she thinks, and then she says, "Let's make it a grande chai latte,

I'm just gonna stop at the coffee place near the studio. And just as I step out of line, the coffee chick raises her eyebrow at me. You know what I'm saying? Like, now we're having a little private moment. And she's kinda cute, despite the nose ring. So I get back in line, intrigued, and that's when the window shatters.

—just collapsed, really. Just, like, smashed and fell into the store like a sheet of water. Like a crashing wave. Crrisshhhh. It was like, crrisshhhh-shishhhhhh. I dropped the coffee I had just made for her. The first one, the half-caf. Dropped it right on the counter, and I guess it must have splashed up.

—and well, of course, I screamed. What am I, not human? I screamed because that bitch just threw a full cup of coffee at me and the front window just shattered and there was a car out at the curb shooting into the coffee shop, Doug.

I covered my head and hit the ground. I heard the shots before the window shattered, so I knew what had happened. Maybe a TEC-9. Or a Glock. Probably a Glock. I know what goes down up here, the gangs and shit. Believe me. I've got a script about it. L.A. gangs in the Valley. It's actually about these kids in the Valley who get so bored being Valley kids that they join a gang. But it's—look, I know, trust me, I've done the research. These gang-bangers don't care if it's eight forty-five in the morning. They don't care that you're at a coffee shop in North Hollywood and not on a street corner in Watts. So I covered my head and hit the half soy, half skim." Like, enough with the halves already. She sees the half-caf in my hand—the one I just poured, for her—and she says, "Hold on a second, Doug," into the phone cord, and then she waves her hand at me and points over at the counter by the urn, and says, "Just put that there. For someone else. Someone else will order that." In that voice. Like, excuse me? Like, I don't know how to do my job? And this has been such a shitty morning so far that it's all I can do to put the half-caf down on the counter and not throw it in her lipsticked face.

As if I've just destroyed her whole little world by changing my mind. God forbid she should take orders from someone without a tattoo. She looked at me as if that coffee was such a waste. Like there were thousands of little Chinese kids going without half-cafs this morning because I decided to order something that cost four times as much. Jesus, Doug. And the guy behind me, some film school wannabe with a goatee and a black knit cap and the whole nine yards, he sighs. He sighs like this is such a burden to him, like I've just increased his time in line by such a monumental amount that he's going to be late for his catering job or his shift at Kinko's or wherever the hell he's off to. And that girl behind the counter sees him sigh, and then she looks at me and raises her eyebrow, like, See? See how much trouble you're causing? I mean, Screw you, right, Doug? Screw you, Goatee Guy, and screw you, Nose Ring.

Nobody was going to budge, not the business lady or the coffee chick. A real standoff. So I think, I'm not gonna wait any longer, ground. I wasn't going out like that. No way. This motherfucker was not going out like that.

I kind of stick my head up a little, and look over the top of the counter, and this kid with a gun just jumps right through the huge hole where the window used to be and runs into the store. He was young—

—maybe fifteen, thirty, eighty-five—how could I tell, Doug? Mexican, maybe? White?

Classic gangbanger. I know the type, I'm telling you.

And all the customers in line had like, hit the deck, so he's running through the store hurdling bodies and he points his gun back at the car by the curb and starts shooting at them through the hole where the window was.

—running right at me, with this gun that he's shooting back over his shoulder. And he says, "Get the fuck out the way, lady"— right, Doug—"out the way," not "out *of* the way"—and then I realized I was the only person in the coffee shop still standing up.

I thought, *Oh shit—that dude is gonna pop a cap in the business lady's ass.*

She was the only one still standing. The kid with the gun was running right at her. I wanted to yell over the counter, like, "Get out of the way, you idiot!" You know? "Get out of the way!" But whoever was in the car was shooting into the store and the kid was shooting outside and you couldn't hear anything except the gunshots and the screaming. So she just stood there, this big coffee stain on the front of her blouse, holding her phone out like a shield.

"Get out the way, lady!" he's yelling. "Get out the motherfucking way!" Doug, what was I supposed to do?

The gangbanger plowed right into her. And they both go down onto the floor in this tangle of arms and legs, and he's trying to get up and away but the business lady's caught in her phone cord—

—and she will not let that goddamned phone go, so she goes back up with him, like, they're tied together at this point—

"Let go," I said. "Let go!" Doug, it was all I could think to say.

The business lady is yelling at him, and the gangbanger grabs her by the front of the shirt, really hard, really rough, and kind of holds her out at arm's length, and, just, without—he doesn't even think twice—he just—

He just pointed the gun at her head—

Doug, what else could I say?

Pow.

He was just a kid, but he had the gun at her head and then he did it.

Doug?

Then the gangbanger was loose and he ran out the back door and the car tore after him. I think they were still shooting. It was hard to tell, my ears were ringing. It was like, Fuck! Did I just see this?

She didn't fall. She just stood there, with her head like that. And she was holding her phone up, out in front of her, like, triumphant. Like she had won—she still had it. The cord was still attached, and the bud was still in her ear. Her mouth was moving, but no sound was coming out.

They were all staring at me like I had two heads, Doug. I thought, *Why are these people staring at me? Why doesn't somebody chase that guy with the gun? Why doesn't somebody do something?*

I got on my phone and called Pat at the studio to tell him what the fuck I had just seen. I figured somebody else was calling the cops.

And there was this pride there, on her face. Even from back behind the counter I could see it. This strength in her body. Like she wasn't going to fall. She was just not going to do it. And then she says—

Doug?

And the coffee chick vaults over the counter and grabs the business lady who is just pumping blood at this point—

She said, "Oh my God this hurts. Oh my God this hurts."

Oh my God this hurts.

It looked like the coffee chick was hugging her. Like they were slow dancing. I was still on the phone, and I could hear the sirens coming.

I would not let her fall.

It was over so quickly, Doug.

You'd better believe they're all going right in that fucking script.

Even though I knew there was nothing.

Doug?

Call it, *The Valley Gangbangers and the Business Lady and the Coffee Chick.*

I would not let her fall.

It was over so quickly.

Jane's Wife

The magnet clung to the door of Liz's refrigerator, what used to be Liz and Jane's refrigerator, front and center, a square needlepoint sampler, with nothing fastened beneath, no shopping list or funny postcard, with no other job than displaying its message, in a voice, Liz imagined, due to the magnet's homespun style, as deadpan, sardonic, Nebraskan, maybe, or Iowan, the bold block letters stitched across its white face in bright blue thread: HAVE ANOTHER SNACK FATTY.

The magnet was a recent purchase, an impulse buy from last week's Rose Bowl Flea Market. Liz had discovered it stuck to a large sheet of brushed metal alongside other magnets with similarly pithy expressions. Seeing it was like making unintentional eye contact with someone she would have liked to avoid, or, more precisely, encountering a deep, unpleasant truth. Once recognized, looking away seemed impossible. It had been made for her. It had been stitched, specifically for Liz, by this kindly, grandmotherly looking lady sitting behind the metal display board thumbing through a copy of *TV Guide*.

Was buying it unnecessary? Was displaying it cruel? Had she nearly doubled in size since the breakup? Not really, but close enough. Liz had gained enough weight in the four months since Jane had been gone that she sure felt doubled, as if she'd stepped into one of those inflatable Halloween fat suits, just to try it on, and couldn't get the damned thing off.

So, yes it was cruel, yes it was grammatically incorrect (where was the comma before the direct address?), but could she honestly look at the body reflected in her (their?) refrigerator door's shine, or the part of her body's reflection that still actually fit in the refrigerator door's shine, and say that the magnet was unnecessary?

Uncurl your fingers from the door handle Fatty. Or, comma, Fatty. Step away from the fridge. Haven't you done enough damage already?

She ran instead of eating lunch. Down the street and across the boulevard, waiting at the light, high-stepping in place, then out into the nicer half of the neighborhood, restored Craftsman homes with German cars in the driveways, moist green lawns, sprinklers spraying rainbows in the sun. Liz was a graceless runner: shambling, breathless, heavy-footed. She had always suspected she was at least a little asthmatic, and her daily turn around the soft grid of streets was beginning to convince her that she may have been right. Running didn't really describe what she did; jogging was the correct term. Whoever had thought of the word was a genius of wicked precision. Every part of her jogged, up, down, right, left, handfuls of flesh bouncing with each sharp step.

Turning a corner, she stumbled to a stop. That dog was there, the blunt, squat, black-and-white lump that was always loose. He stood right in the middle of the street, oblivious. A pine-green pickup loaded with gardening equipment slowed, then inched toward the dog as if to nudge him along. The dog turned, looked up at the pickup's looming grill, then gave out a bratty bark and waddled to the sidewalk. The truck moved on, the driver yelling a curse in Spanish out the open window.

The dog was maybe fifteen feet away. Focusing on Liz now, he bared his teeth. Liz had no idea what kind it was, what breed. She didn't like dogs. When she was eight, she had been bitten by a neighbor's terrier. She still flinched at the thought of that dog's lunge, could still feel his hot breath on her face, the grab and pull. The bite had scarred her, leaving a string of tiny pocks along her left cheek. She had a habit of tapping them with a fingertip, one after another, when she was nervous.

What was this one, a French bulldog? Liz thought she had heard someone, the mailman possibly, describe the dog that way. *That fucking French bulldog is loose again. Chased me half a block.* Fingering the pepper spray clipped to his belt.

What she wouldn't give for her own can of pepper spray. The dog growled, narrowed his gaze. He had a flat-nosed face, white with fat black spots around his eyes. He looked like a cartoon burglar. From somewhere behind the closest house, a little girl's voice called, *Bandit! Bandit!* At least they got the name right.

The dog didn't budge. Liz imagined unclipping a spray can, running forward like a riot cop, reversing a little of her fear. Instead she changed direction, crossing the street to the opposite sidewalk. Jogging unpursued was hard enough.

The jacarandas were flowering, soft blasts of purple cloud along the rooflines. The flowers dropped slowly, a few at a time, sweetening the air. Liz reminded herself to breathe, to keep her head up, force her mouth into a determined smile. Her hope, of course, was that Jane would be driving along for some reason, an errand in the old neighborhood, and see Liz jogging by. The mortification of Jane discovering her new size, which Liz was sure she had already heard about through the long grapevine of mutual friends, would be a worthwhile trade-off for the keen pang of admiration Jane might feel at seeing Liz fighting against her body run amok. As if Liz had reached rock bottom and now there was nowhere to go but up. She could picture Jane's car slowing, Jane's head turning, realizing that she was going to miss it, the struggle and the payoff. It would all be accomplished without her, shared with someone else, maybe, a lucky unknown still out there, waiting to be discovered and included in the victory, the spoils of.

Jesus, her lungs. They felt hot and heavy, like they were full of hardening concrete. The boulevard was in sight again, the end of her little course, but Liz was losing strength by the step. She sputtered, wheezing, bent at the waist, nauseous and dizzy— actually spitting a gob of phlegm down at the curb like a baseball player. Disgusted, disappointed.

There had to be another way to do this. How did people do this? It had been so easy to get fat. That part she had mastered. This part, though. She walked the rest of the way, limping almost, gagging and coughing, finally stopping at the boulevard and waiting for the light to change.

After ten years together, Liz and Jane had married the previous July, during that brief window, that summer of possibilities, after all the talk and debate, the dinner party games, the late night bedroom discussions after a second bottle of wine: Would they if they could, and what would that mean, what would that change? When the court decision came down and it was finally possible, they'd decided to do it, just like that, sitting on the couch watching the news. They would be the first of their friends. That had been important to Jane, to lead the way.

They held the ceremony in Dave and Josh's beautiful backyard in Silver Lake. Kongming lanterns rose to burn in the sunset; a string quartet played Brahms. They even splurged on a honeymoon down to Baja, a week bodyboarding in the ocean and hiking in the hills, touring the blossoming wineries along the inland highway. But nothing had changed, really. That became apparent after the first couple of woozy weeks, once they were home again. The same house, the same discouragements and triggers and resentments. The only difference was that they were official now, card-carrying members in a club of people whose opinion shouldn't have mattered.

Then there was that ecstatic, heartbreaking night in November, the election party at Dave and Josh's, everyone crowded around the TV with the kind of anticipatory anxiety usually reserved for the public confirmation of disaster. When the final presidential returns were announced, the room burst into shouts and cheers of joy and disbelief. Josh sank to the floor, his face covered in tears, and Dave joined him, wrapping his arms around Josh's shoulders, and then everyone joined, as if they couldn't stand upright in the weight of the moment. Liz lay at the bottom of the pile, her eyes closed in the shared warmth.

A voice cut through the celebration then, someone calling out from the kitchen, another TV tuned to another network. Quiet, everybody quiet. The returns were in from Prop 8. The initiative had passed. Marriage had been struck down, struck back. The feeling in the house shifted. Shouted obscenities, more tears. Before Liz could fully realize what was happening, someone was hugging her, someone else was rubbing her back. She looked across the room to find Jane caught in a similar consoling embrace, but when their eyes met Liz didn't see any anger or sadness, only confusion.

What were they now? A clerical anomaly, a historical footnote. Accident survivors, standing beside the wreckage. A strange new group within a group, even more apart from the rest of the world than they had been the day before.

In bed that night they lay awake, not speaking, too stunned by the overload of events. Liz was the first to break. "Now what?" she had said, finally. The words shook the black silence. It was almost like she could see them floating in the air above, sky-written, the letters and question mark bright white and demanding. After a while without any response from Jane, they began to unravel and fade away.

Wet from the post-jog shower, she lay on the bed, avoiding work. The new material from the studio was still in its folder out on the dining room table. Liz didn't have the courage to open it yet. During yesterday's meeting, a low-level producer had asked her how the book was coming and Liz had said, "Great!" with such sudden and artificial enthusiasm that she immediately shut back up and waited for someone at the oblong conference table to call her on her obvious insincerity. But nobody had. They'd all just smiled, happy to cut the meeting short on a high note.

Liz stretched her arms up and out, then pushed her legs down toward the far corners of the mattress. She pictured herself from above, frozen in some kind of naked jumping jack. How many mornings had she woken in this bed? Years of them, now. She and Jane had bought it right after they bought the house. Two thousand mornings. Finding each other across the sheets, hands, lips on necks, on lips, Liz lost in Jane's smell, in her skin. Desire, desired. It had turned by the end, those feelings lost in the final barbed months when they began avoiding contact upon waking, finding the sting from the previous night's argument still there, like another body in between.

They had argued bitterly, the night before Jane left. Liz couldn't even remember the reason, the details. It didn't matter.

The fight was the thing, was the way they communicated now. They had forgotten how to live together any other way.

She had watched as Jane pulled clothes from dresser drawers and shoved them into one of their suitcases.

"Do we even need to get a divorce?" Jane had said.

Liz didn't answer; she didn't have an answer. Jane moved her hands to the top of the dresser, the few pieces of jewelry she owned, a photo of her niece, a bumper sticker from the election just passed. She stopped packing and stared at the sticker.

"They've already decided for us, right?" she said. "One of us just needs to leave."

Dry and dressed, finally. Out in the dining room, Liz shuffled the studio's new material. Other-planetary renderings, mostly— artists' sketches of the alien world, the stark desert landscape, red and brown. Then a few pages of the colonists' settlement, a fantastic, incongruous facsimile of a 1950s suburban tract development, spiraling streets of neat, clean ranch houses in pastel colors shimmering in the heat.

Sketches, script pages, photographs from the set covered the dining room table, the three unoccupied chairs. The movie she was working with was a remake of a big-budget failure from more than thirty years ago, one of the unremembered losers from the late '70s science fiction boom. Liz had never seen the original and the new movie's producers had told her not to bother, that it held no relevance to their updated version.

Whenever she explained her work to someone and received

a slightly pained, uncomprehending look in response, Liz was reminded that this was a strange way to make a living. Books based on movies? Didn't it usually work the other way around?

She had spent the first decade out of college writing her own stories, two kitchen-sink domestic novels that garnered no takers, just some nice and not-so-nice rejections. When her agent had suggested Liz try a novelization, she felt like he was offering her a consolation prize. Jane encouraged her to wait, to keep plugging away at her own work, but Liz had just turned thirty, and the disparity between Jane's success and her own was beginning to wear. Jane had been making a living as an artist for years, exhibiting in shows around L.A., in New York, then Paris, Venice, Prague. Alone with her laptop at the dining room table, Liz had begun to feel like a TV housewife, procrastinating from writing by pushing the vacuum, cleaning the toilet, scrubbing the kitchen sink. Whenever they discussed it, Jane was sympathetic, encouraging. Liz's time would come. She just had to keep working, and refuse to settle. To make light of the imbalance, they made *Donna Reed* jokes, *Ozzie and Harriet* jokes. Jane had even started coming through the door after a day's work, announcing, "Honey, I'm home!" like some impossibly sunny sitcom breadwinner, until Liz asked her, please, to stop.

That was the start of what Liz felt as a gradually increasing separation, the splitting of their *life* into their *lives*. Early on, they'd seen themselves as artists struggling together, a united front against the world. Each one's rejection could be understood and dismissed by the other, used as motivation to try harder. *Fuck 'em*, Jane would say, tearing up another pass from another publisher. But once Jane started to have some success, and Liz's discouragement turned to inertia, the balance began to slide, until it was no longer there at all. Jane was a working artist; Liz was an artist who avoided work. She couldn't help but feel as if she'd been left behind.

Liz ignored Jane's advice and took that first novelization job. The publisher and studio liked her work, and more assignments followed. Spy thrillers, police procedurals, bodice-ripping historical dramas drenched in sweat and palace intrigue. At first she was simply happy to be published. Her name was on the covers; her work was in bookstores, was read, even discussed, sometimes endlessly, on internet forums devoted to the obsessional dissection of every facet of certain film franchises. Some of the books sold well—the ones whose parent pictures became blockbusters or objects of cult worship—and Liz had been able to hold up her end of the mortgage, pay for a vacation or two, the down payments on the cars.

The level of concentration required to write the books surprised her. It was greater even than with her own novels. Liz learned to plumb a depth of imagination she hadn't been aware she possessed. A shooting script might be a hundred pages, but her novelizations needed to be at least two-fifty, so what she was looking for were the unexplored lives, everything said and done off the screenplay page. She enjoyed digging deep into the material she was sent, solving the mystery in it, what the pieces added up to, as if she had been given only ancillary evidence of the real story and now had to divine the truth from the clues.

In those first few years, the only genre she turned down was science fiction. She had never read much of it, didn't think she was attracted by such obvious escapism. All those warp drives and black holes, men going boldly. But during a dry spell she took one on, then another, and those books had become her favorites. Their scripts tended to be so focused on action that Liz found the most open air around them, room to breathe and create. It seemed like the boundaries in these stories were further out, if they existed at all. She could keep pushing, moving further from the center. She could walk into unknown spaces, frightening spaces, exhilarating spaces. These stories were generous, she realized, and open. These stories were all possibility.

Jane had even softened her stance. She hated Hollywood movies, but she read all of Liz's books, some numerous times. I don't need to watch the movies, she told Liz. I don't care what somebody else sees. I'm only interested in your version of the story.

Liz shot out an arm and caught a sketch as it slid south off the table. This was the first job she had taken since the breakup and she was way behind schedule. She had bought herself a little time at the studio meeting, but she needed to get serious, sit down and write, zero in on the script's byzantine plot. Every time she tried, though, she ended up playing around in her notebook, hung up on this one minor character, the unassuming wife of the movie's lead, filling pages with the woman's daydreams and memories, her days alone on the alien planet. The character didn't even have a proper name in the script. She was simply and only, *Dean's*

Wife. Liz knew she was wasting time, sabotaging this job, maybe future jobs, but she felt she was getting close to something, that if she just continued writing, following her slowly unwinding trail of thought, she could describe the woman's fears and desires so completely that she would unlock and release, blooming into a real character, full and round and breathing on the page.

Liz stood and the room tipped, a little hypoglycemic list to the left. Her skipped lunch's revenge. A quick mental inventory of the fridge didn't yield much hope. Last time at the grocery she'd forced herself to buy only what seemed healthy, calorically inoffensive, nonfat yogurt and bags of precut broccoli and carrots. None of it appealed to her now. What she needed was real food, some serious energy, a burger and fries from the grease stand down the street. There was no point torturing herself. She would go get something to eat, then come back and forget about Dean's Wife and knock this thing out. She should run down to the burger place, or at least walk. It was only about a mile away, but the thought of making it down there in her current weakened state and the possibility, however remote, of Jane passing by to see her lumbering down the sidewalk clutching an overstuffed bag of sweet potato fries moved Liz away from her running shoes and back toward the car keys.

She followed the same route she'd just jogged along, relieved to be sitting in the car this time. Driving! What a miracle. Rolling beneath the jacarandas, Liz imagined passing her previous, pathetically clambering self. Feeling a little ashamed actually, as she hit the gas to move on, move past, feeling *judged* if that was possible, by this figment of her own imagination.

She didn't see it, only felt it as she turned the corner: a bump from underneath the car, once, then twice, three times. Liz jumped in her seat with each jolt, then looked into the rearview mirror expecting to see some piece of dislodged machinery in her wake, then thinking, *knowing* almost, that it was the dog. Bandit! She quickly sent out some kind of prayer or wish, hoping it wasn't the dog, and then she saw him, right on cue, standing safely up on the sidewalk, his stubby black-and-white face watching her car pass. Liz loosened her hands from the steering wheel, relieved, looking back up to the rearview mirror, wondering what the hell she had hit, then seeing the reflection at the back of the car, the spin of golden hair, the small body rolling free.

She dialed Jane's number from the police station. They hadn't spoken in weeks, but Liz didn't know who else to call.

Listening to the ring, she kept telling herself that this was her one phone call. But of course it wasn't, she wasn't being charged with anything. This was an accident. The girl was chasing her dog and ran out into the street. Liz may have taken her eyes off the road for a second, less than a second, but that wasn't a crime. You couldn't be punished for inattention.

The girl. Liz could still feel the car bumping once, twice, three times.

She left a message on Jane's voice mail, then sat trembling in a rigid metal chair on the other side of the officer's desk. The man was maybe fifteen years younger than Liz. His neck was crosshatched with tiny cuts and nicks, as if this morning had been his first attempt at shaving. He asked questions and took her answers, his eyes down on his paperwork, as if unwilling to look at her face.

She crossed through the sliding doors into the slick-surfaced corridor, everything straight and flat and scrubbed to a shine, the overhead lights reflecting as bright white suns flashing on the walls, the floor, the polished wood counter of the nurses' station.

The nurse said that she could only give information to the immediate family. She asked Liz if she was immediate family, and Liz said yes. The nurse looked at her for a moment, as if waiting for a different answer, then finally told Liz which corridor to follow. The other family members were back there, the nurse said. The little girl was still in surgery.

The girl's name was Rose. Liz knew this because the girl's father had called it out as he ran toward them in the street.

She walked down the hall, not knowing what to expect, her head full of terrified noise. Turning a corner, she stopped at the edge of a small waiting area. It was softly lit, with carpet and couches and lamps on end tables, like a living room that had been pulled from a house in the neighborhood and dropped into the middle of the hospital.

She saw the father first, that big blond beard. He was wearing the same clothes as when he had come running out to the accident, shorts and a zip-front sweatshirt with the empty hood lolling back between his shoulder blades. Everything was one size too tight, as if he had recently put on weight. He was speaking to an older man, a grayer, slighter version of himself. The father saw Liz and started toward her, his body charged with anger. She thought he was going to take a swing at her. It seemed like the obvious next action. He stopped a step away, still on the carpet.

"What the hell are you doing here?"

He said this clearly, loudly. This was not a private conversation. Liz looked past him into the waiting area. There was the older man and a matching older woman and then a younger woman sitting on the edge of an armchair, her back straight, her hands in her lap. She was the father's age, Liz's age, with lustrous dark hair and large, black-framed glasses. She was dressed smartly, professionally, in a navy-blue blouse and tailored cream pants. She seemed more out of place here than anyone. The father almost belonged, a raw creature stalking the halls, his emotional locks broken, but the mother seemed bewildered, as if at one point in the recent past she had looked up from her desk, expecting to see her workplace, but found herself here instead.

"I'm so sorry," Liz said. "I just didn't—"

"You can't be here," the father said. He was a good head taller, looking down on her, his hands hanging at his sides, fingers stretched out as if he was keeping them from balling into fists. "You need to leave."

Liz stepped back from the carpet. She looked past the father again. The mother and grandparents were watching her. She wanted more than anything to cross into that place, to join their worry and fear.

She couldn't be there. Of course not. But she was a part of it, still. No one would be there if it wasn't for her.

She found a small chapel by the elevators. A square room, no windows, with the same softly glowing lamps as in the waiting area down the hall. There were a couple of wooden kneelers, two chairs, and a coffee table. On the table, a Bible, a Torah, a Qur'an, a paperback copy of *Dianetics*.

She paced the room, not sure what else to do, what physical pose to assume. Standing, sitting, kneeling. She wasn't religious, hadn't been to church since she was a teenager. She pressed her fingertips to the divots on her cheek. The room felt like a cell. The police hadn't confined her, but she would confine herself. She would stay there until something changed, until there was an outcome she would have to face.

She looked through the books on the coffee table. She thought about a book she'd written a few years ago, her favorite so far, a novelization of a movie that, for an enormously complicated and seemingly surreal set of legal and financial reasons, had been shelved at the last minute. Her book, though, for an equally complicated and surreal set of oversights and errors, was still published and shipped to stores. There was only a week or so before all of the copies were recalled, but during that time Liz went to the bookstore at the mall almost every day and stood in the aisle across from its shelf, its cover and spine. It had felt so complete to her, standing there. She knew that she would grieve its loss when it disappeared, but for those few days it existed, and she was happy to be with it, to see its face when she came around the corner. Still there. Not for long; but in that moment, still there.

She checked the time on her phone. When would Jane arrive? When would Jane come in and take control, talk to the doctors, to Rose's parents? Jane had that way of imposing order onto chaos, making sense of the senseless. Liz could imagine it clearly, Jane walking through the chapel door, taking the reins of an unendurable moment.

A sharp point pressed through the pocket of her jeans, into the skin of her thigh. Liz had forgotten about the barrette. After the ambulance had taken Rose and her father, Liz had walked back to her car to get her purse and phone. She was going to leave her car. The police had offered her a ride to the station if she didn't feel capable of driving. She hadn't felt capable. She had found the barrette on the street by the curb. A little metal clasp with a plastic top in the shape of Minnie Mouse's smiling face. Liz had picked it up and looked back to the young police officer with the bad shave. He was waiting for her by his cruiser, but facing the other direction, watching a squawking flock of wild parrots circling above the tree line. Liz had put the barrette in her pocket.

She stood now in the small chapel, moving her fingertips over the smooth curves of Minnie's ears. She could still see Rose lying in the street, her eyes closed as if she were sleeping. It was the only time Liz had ever seen her. Would she ever see her awake? She could picture Rose now, in an operating room down the hall. Lights and machines, tubes and scalpels, men with masks. Rose's face, her eyes closed. The bruises had already started to form when Liz first knelt beside her on the street. Rose's skin darkening, rising in sickening bumps. Liz had never seen her without those bruises, without her body twisted that way.

She should have given the barrette to the police officer. She should have given it to Rose's father. But it felt like it belonged to her now, or that the holding of it belonged to her, its escrow, the waiting.

Down on her knees, Liz pressed her forehead to the tile floor. She felt flushed, feverish, and the tile was cool against her skin. She tried to picture Rose's face smooth and bright, unblemished; her body straight and strong. Tried to imagine her eyes, the color there, what it might be. Blue, sky blue, to go with her sunlit hair. She tried to imagine Rose's eyes opening.

Please. Whispering to the floor, to the operating room down the hall.

Please, wake up.

There was a knock at the chapel door. Liz stood. She didn't know how much time had passed. It was Jane, finally. Jane had come. She wiped her eyes, smoothed her hair, hating herself for her stupid vanity in this of all moments. But Jane had come. Jane was here.

The door opened and an older woman stepped inside. Liz recognized her from the waiting room. Rose's grandmother. But her earlier composure had frayed; a stunned fragility had taken its place. She held her shoulders high and tight, flinch-ready, as if anticipating a blow.

Liz was terrified that she would speak, of what she would say, what news she carried.

What she carried was the smell of cigarettes and a paper plate lined with rolled cold cuts, carrot sticks, florets of broccoli and cauliflower. She looked at Liz and seemed about to say something but then stopped herself.

From out in the hallway, Liz could hear metal carts trundling, the soft bleeping of machines, a distant laugh. A woman's voice over the PA in the hall paged a doctor with a long, consonant-heavy last name.

Liz didn't know what to say, so she didn't say anything. She simply stood there, holding the barrette at her chest. Rose's grandmother looked down at the plate and then back up again, starting over.

She said, "I thought you might be hungry."

Liz slept fitfully, up every hour or so and walking the house, Rose's barrette in her hand.

She checked her phone again. Another missed call from Jane, another voice mail. She didn't listen to the message, but she could still hear Jane's voice, her low honeyed rumble. She looked at Jane's name on the screen and tried to imagine Jane in the house, in this room, her arms around Liz's waist, the new shape of Liz's body, holding her tight. She tried to imagine going through whatever was to come together, carrying this as they had carried so much over the years.

She squeezed Rose's barrette. The pinpoint bit into her skin.

She couldn't do it. Her imagination wasn't strong enough to force Jane into this moment. She belonged to Liz's life before the accident, and now there was this life, whatever it was, whatever it would be. She touched her fingertip to the phone's screen and swiped, erasing Jane's name once, twice, three times.

At the dining room table, she sat and finished the manuscript. She used all of her notes, her sketches, her jogging-route imaginings, every daydream possibility, moving out very far from the center she had been given. She emailed it to her editor, knowing that in a few days she would get a call that it had been rejected, either by the publisher or the studio, or both. It wasn't the book they wanted. It was a book about Dean's Wife, which was something nobody had asked for. But for now, until that call came, it was finished, it felt right.

She checked the clock on the laptop. If she was going to go, it was time. Rose's grandmother had told Liz that the next surgery was scheduled for noon.

The house had grown warmer. The midmorning sun sat hot and white, halfway up the backyard sky. In the kitchen, she packed what she had in the fridge into a canvas grocery bag: little plastic cups of yogurt, a few bottles of water. She left the broccoli and carrots, limp in their drawer. Closing the refrigerator door, she stared at the Fatty magnet for a moment, before pulling it free and setting it up on top of the fridge, just out of reach in the dust and crumbs beside the microwave.

She called a cab. Her car was still in the tow lot. She had no idea if there was any damage. She refused to think about the possibilities, the location of dents, marks on the paint.

How strange to ride a cab through her own neighborhood, like a tourist, someone passing through. Everything looked strange, unrevealed. She winced at every pothole and speed bump. At each stop sign and red light she leaned in to speak to the cabbie, to tell him to turn back, take her home, but before she could make a sound the light would turn, and they'd start forward again.

In the grocery store she filled a cart with boxes of crackers, packages of chocolate-chip cookies, long cardboard cylinders of potato chips in various flavors. Comfort food. It wouldn't be enough. There was no telling how long they'd need to be comforted.

In the toiletries aisle she gathered toothbrushes, toothpaste, face wash. From a rack by the beer she found a pair of men's work pants and a hooded sweatshirt in what seemed like the proper size. When it was her turn at the checkout, the woman at the register asked Liz if she'd found everything she needed, and Liz wanted to say no, to tell the woman that she was going to put it all back, that she didn't want any of it, but instead she pulled her credit card from her wallet and swiped it through the console. Outside, she carried her bags to the waiting cab.

The hospital lot was full, the loading zone lined with ambulances, so the cabbie stopped half a dozen rows back and popped the trunk. Liz paid him and he helped arrange the grocery bags into her arms.

The cab pulled away. Liz started walking through the rows of cars. She reminded herself to breathe, but she couldn't breathe. A flock of birds passed overhead in a loose arrow, then flew out into the distance, above the hilltops; parrots maybe, arcing together in the breeze. She wanted to turn back. She could feel the sun on her neck, on her hands. Keep walking, she told herself, whispering the words aloud. The sound of the whisper seemed like something she could follow, one moment to the next. It was an order, a wish, a prayer. Liz could see Rose's grandmother at the other end of the lot, smoking a cigarette under the hospital entrance overhang. She wanted to stop. She wanted to fall to her knees, drop the heavy bags, unburden herself, allow the contents to spill and roll away, all this stuff she'd bought, too much or not enough. Keep walking, she whispered. She could smell the smoke now, she was that close. She wanted to run off in the other direction, into the street, into traffic, in front of another car, another distracted driver, one of her own. She wanted to scream until the scream filled her head, the parking lot, negating the place, carrying her somewhere, anywhere else. She wanted to turn back.

Instead she whispered again, sending her voice ahead to pull her along.

Golden State

He didn't know anyone. No one knew him. Claire and his mother had moved to Glendora a month into the school year because that's when the lease had run out on their apartment in Utica. Diane didn't have a new job lined up, but she'd inherited a little money when Claire's grandfather died, and she figured they could live off that while she looked. She didn't want to rush into anything; she didn't want to settle this time. She'd told Claire that she was sorry about having to start another new school, that they couldn't have moved later in the year or over the summer, but she didn't want to wait any longer. This was their chance.

Claire didn't know why he'd argued so hard against the move, why he'd yelled and sulked and sniped. It wasn't like there was much to miss in Utica. His dad had left when he was two and Claire had no memory of him and no one had seen the man since. He and Diane had lived in seven different apartments; he'd gone to seven different schools. He was a twelve-year-old boy named Claire with long hair and crooked teeth. A change should do him good, should do them both good. At least, that's what Diane repeated over and over on the drive west, like if she said it enough times out loud it would somehow become true.

Neither of them had been to California before. The only thing Claire knew about the place came from TV, watching the Yankees play the Angels in Anaheim. Back in Utica, the games started late because of the time difference, nine or ten o'clock, but Diane had always let him stay up, even when he was a little kid, spread out in his sleeping bag on the living room floor, watching his team out in the Wild West. Bobby Bonds tracking a fly ball deep into the right field corner and Claire taking his eyes off the play, distracted by the alien background, the strips of freeway crossing the hazy sunset, the long rows of shag-topped palm trees that looked like something out of Dr. Seuss. They may as well have been playing on another planet. The Yanks never did so well out there. Who could blame them?

Diane had used the promise of potential Angels games to help sweeten the deal of the move. Claire had never seen the Yanks play in person, but Glendora was only an hour or so from Anaheim, and when summer came, Diane said, she'd find a way to get them to a game. He imagined a spot in the right field bleachers, watching Bonds running down a fly, both he and Bobby turning their heads at the last moment to look out over that foreign terrain beyond the wall. Catch, cheer, maybe their eyes meeting in silent recognition. Men of New York. Bobby, though, would get to go back home after the game.

Their new street in Glendora ran long and wide along the base of the lower San Gabriels. The sight of the broad mountains filled Claire's bedroom window. Diane said that plenty of people would kill for that view, but it was obvious, based on the ages and conditions, that the homes on the other side of the street were the real prizes. They boasted long, smooth, newly paved approaches, driveways like lavish greetings. Big and new and beautiful, those houses stood with the mountains at their backs, as if facing out together, powerful and confident. The neighbors directly across the street had the most impressive spread of all, a broad sweep of gleaming blacktop that stretched back to a white Spanish-style home with an orange tile roof and a two-car garage.

The place Claire and Diane were renting was a beige shrug of a house, a short wooden shoebox with a square patch of dirt and weeds for the front lawn, a stub of buckled concrete driveway barely long enough for their tired green Corolla. Security bars covered the windows and there was a heavy metal screen bolted over the front door, though Claire wasn't sure who they were trying to keep out. Their wealthy neighbors?

The neighbors across the street, those of the incredible driveway and fancy villa, as Diane called it, were named the Bartletts. Claire knew this because it was spelled out along the side of their huge stainless steel mailbox, one reflective metallic sticker for each letter, so that when a car's headlights passed at night Claire could see the name appear in the dark from his bedroom window, the letters flashing quickly white. *Bartlett!*

Like the *Quotations*, Diane said. It's a big book, she told him, with famous sayings by famous people. Most of them dead.

Claire had called his mom Diane since he was four, when he'd first discovered her real name. Over the years, plenty of adults had tried to correct him, teachers and his grandparents, some of Diane's boyfriends. But he'd stuck to it. He preferred *Diane* to *Mom*. It bound her to him, specifically. Everyone had a *Mom*, but only Claire had *Diane*.

"Give me a quote," Diane said. They were having breakfast at the kitchen table. Frosted Flakes and toast and the newspaper classifieds. She'd already started looking for a job. The inheritance money had gone faster than expected. Much of it had been eaten by the move itself, and everything else was so much more expensive out here, rent and groceries and gas.

Diane said, "Give me the most famous quote you can think of." She loved riddles, quizzes, puzzles. She loved a good test.

" '*Ask not what your country can do for you,*' " Claire said.

"Excellent. Definitely in *Bartlett's*."

"Your turn."

Diane thought for a second. She set the job listings down, tilted her head back, chin up.

"Herbert Hoover had a good one," she said. " '*About the time we think we can make ends meet, somebody moves the ends.*' "

The central, unavoidable feature of Claire's new bedroom was the wallpaper some previous tenant had left behind, a giant floor-to-ceiling photo of a beach scene, sunset over the water, or maybe sunrise, depending on where he was standing, as the same paper covered two opposite walls. Claire added what he'd brought along, a Yankees pennant, an Ozzy Osbourne poster, a few pictures he'd cut out from dirt bike magazines. Diane had hammered a couple of nails above the window and hung one of Claire's old bed sheets to cover it. H.R. Pufnstuf, the big yellow puppet smiling and waving in front of a psychedelic rainbow swirl. Claire remembered the sheet mostly for wetting it, waking up long ago in the middle of the night, one of their old apartments, Diane stripping the bed in the dark while he stood by, shivering and crying, Diane telling him it was all right, just an accident, everybody makes mistakes.

The Bartletts spent most of their days outside, so it wasn't like Claire was spying on them, more just watching whatever was happening out his window. Mrs. Bartlett was a tall, tan woman with crayon yellow hair, skinny except in her bust and hips. She worked long hours in her front yard, trimming the hedges that bordered the bright, short grass; clipping roses; weeding out the beds of wildflowers and prickly cactus that curved through the lawn in long, gentle swoops. While his wife worked in the yard, Mr. Bartlett worked on his pickup, a big, new-model Ford with a pale blue finish that almost perfectly matched the sky above the San Gabriels. He looked like a cowboy, stood and walked like a cowboy, wide-stanced, tall and trim in checkered western shirts and faded jeans, with a generous mustache that obscured most of his mouth and the top of his chin.

The other kids on the street, all crew-cut boys, had no interest in Claire except as an object of sneering condescension—*Hey, hippie!*—but they had a lot to say about Mrs. Bartlett, who often did her yard work wearing a red-and-white-striped bikini. The boy who lived three houses down from the Bartletts liked to tell stories of clandestine, binoculared viewings of Mrs. B. sunbathing topless on a chaise in her backyard, the details offered in the back of the school bus drawn out for maximum erotic effect: Mrs. Bartlett rolling slowly from her belly to her back, brown skin slick with baby oil. Mr. Bartlett was pretty cool, the boys said, which was how he'd gotten such a foxy wife. He was a guitarist, an *electric* guitarist, who played on all sorts of records for singers who didn't have their own bands and for already famous bands that had really bad guitarists.

The Bartletts had twin sons, but they were grown and lived away upstate. They'd left some legends behind, though, and the boys on Claire's bus, the younger brothers of the Bartlett twins' contemporaries, told these stories with all the required reverence due to great mythic narratives. There was the time the Bartletts did battle with a pack of coyotes down from the mountains, scaring away the rangy beasts with hockey sticks and baseball bats. There was the time they shot a bottle rocket so high on the Fourth of July that it hit the underside of a TV helicopter. There was the time they built a plywood ramp in the middle of the street, backing up traffic as they rode their bikes over and off until the cops came and made them take it down.

Claire listened, beguiled by the amazing tales. But he understood the intention with which they were told, the message being sent: this history belonged to these boys. Claire could be impressed, but it wasn't his to share. They made it very clear that

he was a visitor here. This wasn't his place, and these weren't
his stories.

"Why California?" Claire had asked, back when Diane first
announced the move.

"Why not?" she'd said. "That pioneer spirit. Leaving the old
world behind. And it's the Bicentennial. What better way to cel-
ebrate our independence? Westward ho!"

But there were plenty of places to move where she could wait
tables or answer phones. Claire knew that Diane had picked California because of *The Price Is Right*. Not in terms of the cost of
living, but rather the actual television game show starring Bob
Barker. Diane's deepest desire was to be a contestant, seated anx-
iously in the audience, waiting for Bob to call out for her to *Come
on down!* She dreamt of that run down the aisle steps, waving
her arms in the air, shouting with joy, her oversized name tag
bouncing along as she descended toward the stage. And not just
the usual daydreams, she'd told Claire, but real honest-to-God
dreams in the night now, coming unbidden into her sleeping head.

"It's a sign," she'd said. "Don't you think? When you're
having real dreams, it's time to stop wishing. It's time to act."

But why Glendora, out of the seemingly millions of possible
L.A. suburbs? Why not Lakewood or Sylmar or the intriguingly
futuristic-sounding Panorama City?

Listen to it, she'd said when he'd asked. Listen to the word.
Glendora. How beautiful. How magical. It sounds like the Good
Witch on the way to Oz.

Claire wasn't so sure. This wasn't what he'd expected. Where was the Los Angeles of *The Brady Bunch* or *The Partridge Family*, the lush endless TV suburb? Instead they'd found a hot, dry place, with a sharp tang in the air that wasn't the sea salt he'd first foolishly thought, but car exhaust, stuck here hanging at the foothills, unable to rise and escape. And the mountains—no one had said there'd be mountains. They were so close they made him dizzy. They filled his vision, sloped and shadowed, folded like great mounds of crumpled paper. Even when he wasn't looking, he could feel their looming presence, setting the neighborhood off balance, threatening to tip the whole place from the unequal distribution of weight, as if just a few more pounds crossing the street would be enough for everything to swing.

It was the first of November but still rainless, warm even in the overnight hours. He slept with just a sheet on top of him. He'd always imagined mountains as snow-capped, but these were copper-headed, covered with dry tinderbox grass. There were fires farther down the range. At night he could hear the air tankers buzzing through the darkness, racing to drop water, then passing back overhead to suck more from the reservoir. He left his window open, pictured the Bartletts' yard: cool, green, teeming with foliage. Sometimes in the early hours their sprinklers would burst on, waking him halfway, and he'd lie in the dark for a few moments before falling back asleep, listening to the flickering spray, his room growing cooler with the sound.

* * *

He was walking home from the bus stop when Mr. Bartlett called him over. Claire and the other boys all did confused double and triple takes as to whom the cowboy was talking to. "My new neighbor," Mr. Bartlett called out, to confirm. He was standing at the end of his driveway, by the open door of his idling pickup.

Claire jogged across the street, feeling the daggers stared into his back by the boys continuing on to their own houses, feeling his own anxious knife points in his gut. Had he been caught staring out his window at Mrs. Bartlett?

Claire reached the end of the driveway and Mr. Bartlett extended a hand. Claire took it, shook.

"Bruce Bartlett," Mr. Bartlett said. "Bruce to you. My wife Tammy's inside. We've been meaning to introduce ourselves."

"I've been admiring your truck," Claire said, nodding back across the street to his own house, his bedroom window, attempting a little preemptive ass-covering.

"She is a beauty. Remind me sometime and I'll give you a ride." Bruce looked across the street. "Who's living with you there? Your mother?"

"Diane," Claire said.

"That's it?"

Claire nodded.

"We have two boys ourselves. Up raising hell in Bakersfield now." He turned back to Claire. "Tell you what. You want to earn some money sometime, you come on over and I'll set you up washing and waxing the truck. Then we can drive it into town and show it off. Sound good?"

"Yes, sir," Claire said.

"Good man." Bruce clapped him on the shoulder, got into the cab of the pickup.

Claire was halfway across the street when Bruce called to him again.

"Didn't get your name, son."

Claire had the urge to shout back something harder, more masculine, Greg or Derrick or Jake. He thought better of it, though, the other boys were still watching from their own driveways, so he yelled out his name, but it was right in time with an engine rev from Bruce's pickup, so he had to do it again, louder this time, his voice cracking as he called out from the middle of the street.

"Claire!"

"A dollar and twenty-nine cents. Seventy-nine cents. Two and a quarter."

Just before dinnertime, but it was an artificially overlit high noon in the canned soup and vegetable aisle of the Ralphs supermarket on Glendora's eastern edge. Claire pushed the cart and Diane called out prices without looking as Claire named items on the shelves. This was how she kept in shape for *The Price Is Right*. Same routine when she saw a commercial on TV. Sometimes in the evening they watched just for the commercials, eating dinner off tray tables on the couch, keeping the sound down and talking during *All in the Family* or *McMillan & Wife* but getting serious when the ads started, Claire crossing the room to raise the volume while Diane called out prices.

"Sixty-two cents."

"Negative." Their cart had a wonky front wheel, and Claire had to muscle it forward to keep from drifting into the shelves.

"Campbell's Cream of Potato Soup is sixty-two cents," Diane said.

"Sixty-five cents."

"Jesus. Really? Price hike."

Claire dropped the can into their cart, picked at a zit that had surfaced in the center of his chin. "I talked to Bruce Bartlett the other day."

"Is that a kid at school?"

"He's our neighbor. Across the street."

"With the villa?"

"Green Giant Corn Niblets."

"Fifty-eight cents."

Claire nodded, dropped the can into their cart. "He seemed okay. Bruce. Said he'd pay me to wash his truck sometime."

"How generous."

"It's a nice truck."

"He should tell his wife to put some clothes on."

"Wattie's Diced Fruit Salad."

"Fifty-three cents," Diane said. "Always."

"When are you going to go over and get in line?"

"When we're done shopping."

"I mean at *The Price Is Right*. The audience line."

"They're running a contest," Diane said. "Johnny Olson announced it during the credits the other day. You call in and tell them why you're the show's biggest fan. If they pick you, you get a VIP place in the line."

"And you'd get on?"

She shook her head. "They didn't say that. You'd just have a better chance, I guess."

Claire jockeyed the cart into a checkout aisle, started handing groceries to the woman at the register. "So when are you going to call?"

"It's not the right time." Diane dug into her purse for cash. Kept digging. "We need to get settled, get our feet under us. I need to get a job."

"You're scared."

"We have all the time in the world. We're here now."

"You told me it's time to act."

Diane smiled at the woman behind the register, handed her the money for the groceries, a wrinkled sheaf of small bills with a halo of change. "I'll think about it."

"'The only thing we have to fear . . .'"

"Yeah, yeah." Diane hefted a grocery bag over to Claire. "I've heard that line before."

He washed and waxed the truck, eating up most of a Saturday morning in the Bartletts' driveway, jeans and T-shirt wet from the hose, Chuck Taylors soaked and squeaking with every step. Bruce had given Claire very detailed instructions, then he and Mrs. Bartlett had taken off in her car, a little red Fiat with a removable hard top they'd left propped against a wall in the garage on their way out.

When he was finished with the truck, Claire sat back on the edge of the front porch, stretching his legs onto the driveway, drying his shoes in the sun. The porch was made of large flat slabs of concrete, painted a color that resembled the warm red brick of his grandparents' house back in Utica. The paint was smooth as a cheek. He ran his hand along the top, thought about leaning over and setting his own cheek against it, wondering how that would feel. It felt soft, and warm from the sun. He closed his eyes, his cheek against the paint. He thought of the house in Utica, coming up the front walk, his grandfather waiting in the doorway.

He heard the Fiat before he saw it, howling down the street and then taking the turn into the driveway so tightly that Bruce, sitting in the passenger seat, had to grab the top of the door to keep from tumbling out. Mrs. Bartlett hit the brakes just a few inches shy of the newly shined pickup, threw open the door and stalked to the front door of the house in her halter top and cutoffs, right past Claire, now sitting upright on the edge of the porch, her bare thighs just an inch or two from the side of his face as she passed.

Bruce sat in the car for a moment, then collected himself and got out, closing his door and crossing around to the other side to close hers. He gave Claire a tight-lipped smile, then began inspecting the pickup, face close to the finish, studying the wax job.

Claire stood, pulling his wet jeans from where they'd stuck to his thighs. He started winding the hose. He could hear Mrs. Bartlett back in the house, what sounded like kitchen cabinets slamming shut. Bruce ignored the noise. He picked one of the dry rags out of Claire's bucket and buffed a few spots around the headlights, the front bumper.

"Not bad at all." He dropped the rag back in the bucket, turned to Claire. "What price did we agree on?"

"We didn't."

"You're a terrible negotiator. How about a buck?"

"Okay."

"Don't let me off so easy. This is a buck and a quarter job, at least." Bruce reached into the back pocket of his jeans for his wallet, then let his hand drop. "How about this. I'll come up with an invoice. One twenty-five for the truck, another dollar if you do Tammy's car tomorrow. Ten cents a day if you bring the paper up the driveway in the morning before school. That's two seventy-five, and I'll pay you on Friday. Every Friday. What do you think?"

Claire nodded.

"You drive a hard bargain." Bruce's mustache bowed up in a smile. He stepped to Claire. He was a good half-foot taller, Claire at eye level with his mustache. His breath was sour with beer. Claire could hear the slamming of doors inside the house, a quick succession, popping like TV gunshots.

Bruce's smile stayed steady, not without some apparent effort. He extended his hand and Claire took it.

"You're hired," Bruce said.

At lunchtime, Claire went down to the faculty lounge under the pretense of finding his science teacher, who he knew was on yard duty at the time. The gym coach told him that he could hang out and wait, so Claire casually flipped on the TV by the toaster oven and switched it to *The Price Is Right*. The gym coach looked at the TV and then went back to his sandwich. Once Johnny Olson had announced the phone number for the audience contest, Claire headed out to the pay phone just inside the main entrance, dug for a dime, dialed.

"She's the biggest fan by far," he explained to the woman on the other end of the line, spelling Diane's full name and giving their new phone number. The woman asked him to elaborate. Why *The Price Is Right*?

"Because you have to know things to win," Claire said. He turned to see the gym coach coming his way, frowning. "It's not just luck. You have to make it happen."

The woman said she had one more question. The gym coach was coming faster, slicing his hand back and forth under his chin, telling Claire to cut the call.

What do you think is the craziest thing, the woman asked, that your mother would do to be on the show?

"She's already done it," Claire said. The gym coach arrived, his finger stretching toward the phone's hookswitch. "We moved all the way from New York for this."

There was something wrong with the toilet. It was slow to flush, and had the ugly habit of coughing up parts of whatever had just been sent down. Diane had left a few phone messages for the landlord, asking for a plumber, but hadn't heard back yet.

Claire looked down into the bowl, called out to the kitchen.
"Diane!"

"It's just got heartburn, honey," Diane yelled back. "Make it swallow again."

"Gross."

"Plunge it, Claire. Give it a good plunge."

Out in the hall closet, Claire stood looking in at the tangled mess of Diane's clothes and shoes, boxes of tax returns and bank statements and charge card bills, shelves of bath towels, bed sheets, toilet paper, cleaning supplies. It was the only closet in the house, besides the one in Claire's room. "I will sacrifice," Diane had said when they'd moved in, "so you can have the front room. But no complaints about this closet. Everything has to fit in here." Or maybe she just hadn't wanted the room with the wallpaper.

Claire started digging. There was no sign of the plunger, but Diane's jewelry box was there, on the floor beside the paper towels. The box had been a gift from Claire's grandfather, who'd made wooden puzzle boxes on his days off from the meat market. Each one was different, and each contained a hidden panel that had to be pressed before the front drawers would open. Claire had spent entire afternoons in his grandfather's basement, trying to solve every box on the workbench.

This one had a floral carving on top, three sunflowers stretching for the sky. The button was concealed within one of the petals ringing the center flower's face. Claire pressed it and opened the top drawer. All the familiar treasures were there:

Diane's plain gold wedding band, a pair of earrings she'd been given long ago by a high school boyfriend, a colored glass Santa Claus brooch she wore around the holidays. A square of folded paper was there, too, which was new, and which Claire couldn't stop himself from opening. It was a long letter to Diane, dated a couple of months back, just before the move. Two pages, neatly printed, from someone named Steve. Claire scanned rather than read, worried that Diane would come around the corner any second. The gist of the letter was how thrilled Steve was that he'd soon see Diane again after all these years. That he'd changed a lot since high school, of course. He was sure she had, too. A lot had happened, but that meant they were wiser now, not just older. There was a Los Angeles address and phone number, a P.S. asking her not to wait too long to call once she was settled out west.

"Claire?" Diane's voice called out from the kitchen.

Claire refolded the letter, stuffed it back in the box. He stood too quickly, bumping a roll of TP off a high shelf, triggering more rolls, falling slowly at first, then gathering speed, an avalanche of unfurling paper. He tried to catch them as they tumbled, or at least deflect them from his face.

"Did you get it to flush?" Diane called. "Claire, is it going down?"

Claire washed and waxed Bruce's truck and Tammy's car every weekend, delivered the paper in the mornings before school, drew up an invoice at the end of each week listing everything he'd done and the accompanying price. On Friday afternoons when he got home from school, an envelope was waiting for him, wedged between the front door and the security gate, cash and exact change inside, along with the invoice, each item checked off and the bottom signed by Bruce.

On Thanksgiving, while Diane was cooking the turkey, they watched the Macy's parade on TV, just like every year, except here the incongruity between the blustery weather onscreen and the dry sunny scene out the open windows was jarring, and Claire kept looking from one bright square to another, trying to piece together the space between the two.

They had dinner early, as Diane had found a job doing laundry at Foothill Presbyterian Hospital, and had to work the evening shift. She wore her new green scrubs at the table, which made her look like a nurse, and Claire remembered that she'd once talked about becoming a nurse, years ago, had even taken some classes, maybe. He had vague memories of Diane dropping him off with his grandparents before dinner so she could go to school. He didn't say anything about this at dinner though, and he didn't ask about Steve, the writer of the note he'd found, though there had been numerous times he'd wanted to. Had she called him yet? Had they seen each other? Claire kept checking the puzzle box in the hall closet for the note, as if its disappearance would mean that something was in motion. He knew nothing about the guy's life, or about Diane's time with him, but looking at the note was comforting. There was someone who was aware of them, who knew they were here.

The next morning, Claire woke to find Bruce's envelope wedged into the front door. Inside was that week's job list crossed out and paid for, and then, rattling around at the bottom of the envelope, an additional dollar, four shiny new Bicentennial quarters, itemized on the invoice in Bruce's handwriting, right above his signature, as *Holiday Bonus*.

That Saturday, Claire was finishing up the wax on Bruce's truck, when the shouting began again from the house behind him, Bruce and Tammy's voices, the words indecipherable but the tone and tenor familiar by now, moving through the rooms. Claire imagined the collective sound as a ball of light, a freeze-framed explosion, jagged orange and yellow at its points but white hot in the center. He almost expected to see its glow as it passed by the front windows. He kept waiting for it to give, to blow free, unleashing a supernova, the Big Bang.

Bruce smacked the screen door open and crossed the front yard, carrying a beer. When he finished the last swallow, it looked to Claire like he was about to toss the can into one of Tammy's manicured poppy beds, but then he changed his mind and set it down with overdeliberate care, upright, exactly on the border between the lawn and the driveway. He dug into his jeans for his keys, kicked the hose out of his way, nodded to the passenger side, told Claire to get in.

They headed down Foothill Boulevard, driving west into the low afternoon sun. Bruce was quiet, decompressing. Claire noticed a dull spot on the dash and used the bottom of his T-shirt to rub it to a shine. They rode alongside the freeway, then turned south and crossed underneath.

"What do you listen to?" Bruce said, breaking the silence. "In terms of music."

Claire chewed the nail on an index finger, peeling slivers of car wax with his teeth. "Black Sabbath," he said. "AC/DC. Judas Priest."

Bruce nodded, contemplating, maybe judging the guitar abilities of Tony Iommi and Angus Young and K.K. Downing.

"Christ," he said finally. "I feel old sometimes."

At the sign for the racetrack, Bruce turned into the enormous, empty parking lot. The marquee by the main entrance said that races would resume after Christmas. Bruce stopped the truck in the middle of an aisle, left it running, got out and stood looking back in at Claire.

"Slide over."

Claire scooched behind the wheel. Bruce crossed around the front of the truck and climbed up into the passenger seat.

"You ever driven stick before?"

"I've never driven anything before."

"The pedal on your left is the clutch. Brake in the middle, gas on the right. Keep one foot on the brake and the other on the clutch and put it in first."

Claire maneuvered the truck through the lot, ten, fifteen miles an hour, stalling out a few times but slowly gaining confidence, finding the rhythm, his feet pushing pedals. Eventually he kept the engine going long enough that Bruce started calling out,

Clutch! when they hadn't stalled and Claire would shift up, their speed increasing, his hair blowing back from the open windows, Bruce shouting, *Clutch!*, the truck going faster, Claire making turns up and down the aisles, trying for some reason to hold back a smile that wouldn't be suppressed.

They drove until the sun was down, Claire controlling everything by the end, Bruce sitting back in his seat with his hands laced behind his head and his eyes closed. There was a tattoo on the inside of his right forearm, a single blue word, *Tammy*. Claire drove, listened to the music. Bruce had put a cassette in the deck, a country and western band with pretty intricate guitar work, no vocals. Claire kept thinking he should ask if that was Bruce playing, but he felt like he probably knew the answer and he didn't want to disrupt the sound of the engine and the music. They went together, they fit, and he knew a voice would ruin it, breaking the spell, like putting his finger into one of the soap bubbles when he was washing the cars, a little domed rainbow, something beautiful and fragile and gone.

Diane was home late, tired, her third double shift that week, trying to throw some dinner together in the kitchen. Claire was leaning in the doorway, telling her about his day at school, when the phone rang.

Claire answered, listened, covered the mouthpiece with his hand.

"Holy shit."

Diane turned on him. "What did you say?"

"I said, 'Holy shit.' It's somebody from CBS."

Diane wiped her hands with a dishtowel, approached warily. "If you're pulling my leg, I'll wring your neck."

He handed her the phone.

"Hello?" she said. "Yes, speaking."

Claire watched, his stomach doing sudden somersaults.

"Yes," Diane said. "Let me get a pen." She motioned frantically to Claire and he searched the kitchen in a panic, finally coming up with a broken stump of bowling pencil and a Ralphs receipt. Diane began writing directions on the back of the receipt. At the bottom she wrote, *CBS Television City*, and underlined it twice, emphatically.

When she hung up the phone they stood in silence for a moment, the air in the kitchen charged, expectant. Then Diane said, "Holy shit is right," and they were both yelling, jumping, holding hands, dancing around the kitchen, Claire shouting, "Come on down! Come on down!" and Diane making loud whoops, like some kind of ecstatic security alarm, shaking the plates in the dish drainer, rattling the utensils in the drawers, letting the water in the pot on the stove boil and bubble and overflow.

A few nights later, Diane had a date. She didn't call it a date, she said that she was going to have dinner with an old friend, but while she was getting ready in her bedroom, Claire checked the puzzle box and the note from Steve was gone. He wondered who had called whom. Maybe the phone call from CBS had given Diane the confidence to finally make her move.

She came out of her room wearing a dress Claire had never seen before. Not new, necessarily, but new to Diane. Pale blue, not unlike the color of Bruce's truck, and short, ending just above her knees. It had a zipper on the back that Claire had to help with, moving the slider up between Diane's freckled shoulder blades to the base of her neck.

They walked out the front door together and Diane gave him a list of instructions, even lengthier than usual: not to open the door for anybody, how long to cook the frozen egg rolls for dinner, when to go to bed if she wasn't home. She kissed him on the cheek and headed for the Corolla. She smelled like flowers. She was wearing perfume. Claire waved as she backed out of the driveway, then waved again when he saw Bruce and Tammy in their front yard. Tammy was wearing a low-cut sundress, the same artificial color as her hair. Yellow #5, Diane called it. One of the ingredients in Froot Loops.

Bruce was staring back at Claire, but it was hard to tell if he saw the wave. He was just listening as Tammy spoke in what looked like hard, clipped bursts. Bruce said something back to her, then turned and walked up the lawn, gesturing angrily as he went, brushing his hands together, wiping them clean.

When Diane got home late that night, she was singing. Claire lay in bed, listening as she moved through the dark house. The sound of her heels clicking across the floors, water run-

ning in the bathroom sink. Her soft, high, off-key voice drifting between rooms, singing the lyrics when she remembered
them and humming the tune when she didn't, a medley of songs
Claire knew from the radio on his grandfather's old workbench, "You'd Be So Nice to Come Home To," "You'd Be So
Easy to Love."

A kid named Jay was selling his bike. Word went around on the
bus, but there wasn't much interest. Everyone seemed to know
the bike in question. Claire approached Jay on the walk home,
and Jay led Claire to his house, another Spanish-style villa on
Bruce's side of the street.

Jay had a crew cut, like every other boy in the neighborhood,
but he also had a harelip, a stark crooked thumbprint in the skin
below his nose. The first time Claire had seen Jay on the bus,
he'd hoped, because of the lip, that Jay might be more open than
the other kids; looking for a friend, maybe. But that wasn't the
case. For the most part, he ignored Claire. He was a leader, one
of the guys who called the shots at school and on the bus, carrying himself with an exaggerated physical pride, the harelip not
a cosmetic blemish but a scar, like a war injury, something he'd
earned.

On the walk up his driveway, Jay made sure Claire knew that
this was his second bike, his beater, the bike he used for stunts and
hard riding up in the foothills. His other bike was a two-hundred-
dollar Mongoose that he kept in the garage, beside his father's
Mercedes. The beater he kept out on the side lawn.

"The seat is a little loose," Jay warned, "and the back brakes don't work, only the front, so if you stop too hard you'll flip over the handlebars."

The garage door was open, and Claire could see the Mongoose and Mercedes inside. The Mercedes had a sticker on its back bumper that read, WIN WITH FORD!, which seemed strange until Claire realized that it referred to the president, not the car company.

Jay took Claire around to the side of the house, pointed down into the grass. Lying there was a Frankenstein's monster of a bike, a mishmash of parts from other models, everything slightly out of proportion to everything else. The front tire had a mag rim, the back tire had spokes. The frame was painted primer gray, like there was another color waiting that had never been applied. Claire asked how much Jay wanted for it and Jay said ten dollars. Claire countered with five. Jay scoffed, insulted, but after a moment he looked back at the bike and let out a sigh and said, Okay.

Claire paid with four dollars in bills, one more in Bicentennial quarters. Jay looked at the coins like he wasn't sure what they were, like it was play money. He finally put it all in his pocket and nodded to the bike.

Claire rode it home, turning sine curves along the width of the street, thinking of the Bartlett twins, their legendary ramp in the middle of the road. When he got to their house, Bruce was in the driveway, getting into his truck. He looked at Claire on the bike and smiled.

"Guess how much," Claire shouted.

Bruce put his hands on his hips, appraising the bike as Claire turned in a circular holding pattern at the end of the drive.

"Eight bucks."

"Five!" Claire shouted, pulling a wheelie, pedaling through, off and away down the street.

When Diane wasn't working and Claire wasn't at school, they were in Ralphs, or Sears, or Thrifty, walking the aisles, Claire pointing out random items and Diane giving the price. Sometimes Claire gave her a number just off the actual retail value and Diane had to determine if he was high or low. On days when Diane had to work the night shift, they went early, before school, Claire waking to find Diane standing at the foot of his bed in the low light, shaking his bare foot, calling out like a drill sergeant, "Let's go, let's go, Hinshaw's opens at seven!"

Diane had a second date, which meant another almost-new dress, another perfumed goodbye in the driveway. When she was gone, Claire went back inside and opened the puzzle box. The note from Steve was there again, and Claire sat in the hallway and read it more carefully. Steve wrote that he'd lived in Hollywood for about ten years, working as a gaffer on movie sets, which meant that he set up the lights. It wasn't as glamorous as it might seem, he wrote, though he'd worked with his share of movie stars. He had two kids, a boy and a girl, right about Claire's age, though they lived with their mother back east and he rarely saw them.

He was divorced, of course, couldn't remember why'd he'd gotten married in the first place. Young and foolish, he guessed. He wrote that it seemed he and Diane had made many of the same mistakes.

When Diane got home that night she was singing again, a little louder this time. Claire wondered if she was drunk. He got up and joined her in the kitchen. She still smelled of perfume, though she smelled of smoke now, too, the sweet, peaty scent of a cigar, so Claire added that to his mental picture of Steve, a burning stogie clamped between the man's teeth.

Diane stood at the end of the kitchen, taking her vitamin with a glass of water. She looked at Claire in his pajamas, smiled.

"My little boy's not much of a boy anymore," she said.

She finished her water, set her glass in the sink and walked to the doorway, slowing to kiss Claire's cheek as she passed. A light brush of lips, sticky on his skin. She went down to the bathroom and closed the door. Claire could hear the water running. He returned to bed, realizing as he fell back asleep that, without her shoes, Diane now needed to stretch up on her toes to reach him.

Claire was in the driveway working on his bike when Bruce called him over.

"I'm raking around the old oak. Come and give me a hand."

Bruce handed Claire a pair of gloves and a metal rake and they walked around to the backyard, which was even larger than the front, a great swath of manicured green that ran up to the first slope of the foothills. That dizzy feeling was even stronger here, so close to the towering mountains. Claire felt for a moment like he was about to tip, like the axis of the world was the low wall of river rock at the edge of the Bartletts' yard, that everything could swing one way or another around that line. He focused on the wall to regain his balance, the smooth gray stones with their deep red veins. Little planets, they looked like. Dead worlds, dried up and uninhabitable, stacked here in counterbalance to the mountains.

"Hey, space cadet," Bruce called. "Let's get to work."

The big oak stood in the center of the yard, curved and gnarled and shedding crisp leaves even as they raked beneath it. There had been winds the last few days, warm dry breaths in the afternoons and evenings, what Bruce called the Santa Anas, the devil winds, which made people crazy and brought the coyotes down from the mountains.

"See that light?" Bruce said. He'd stopped raking and stood with his arms out, the late afternoon sun falling on his bare forearms. "You don't get that anywhere but here. That quality. The smog holds the sunset in the air. You can almost feel it in your body." He closed his eyes. "It changes how you feel."

Claire watched Bruce. He looked peaceful, maybe even happy, standing there in the orange light. He looked like he belonged here, in this strange, rough landscape, under his tree, beside his mountains. Claire closed his own eyes and slowly lifted his arms, trying to feel what Bruce felt, tried to feel his body as a part of this place, this light, but then Bruce coughed and Claire snapped his eyes open, embarrassed, coughing in response to try to clear the moment.

They raked in silence for a while, just the sound of the leaves scraping across the grass, and then Bruce spoke again from the other side of the tree.

"Seeing you with that bike reminded me of my boys. They were always on their bikes, always jumping over things, off things." He pulled his leaves into a single low pile. "I haven't seen them in I don't know how long. They've got their own lives now." He set his rake against the trunk and looked down at their work. "I can handle the rest. You go on back. Make sure you put this on your invoice."

When Claire got home he found the phone cord stretched through the kitchen and out the back door. He could see the top of Diane's head through the window. She was sitting on the back steps. Her voice was muffled, but it was obvious that she was arguing. No, no, you listen. You listen to me now. He heard Steve's name, said in anger, said as a kind of plea. Steve, listen to me. Steve, why is this happening again?

When Diane came back inside she was carrying the receiver like it was a dead animal, the handset held away from her body. Claire started washing the dishes in the sink to make it look like he hadn't been eavesdropping.

Diane said, "Since when do you wash dishes?"

Claire shrugged.

"Don't think you're going to give me an invoice like Bruce Bartlett."

She left the kitchen. Claire could hear her in the hall closet, then back in her bedroom. He didn't know why he suddenly felt so knocked back by this. Diane had had breakups before. Every relationship she'd been in had ended in a breakup. And Claire hadn't even met Steve. Steve hadn't taken him bowling or to the movies or the dirt bike races like some of the other boyfriends, as if auditioning for a part in their little family show. Steve was just a name on a letter. He wasn't anything real.

After a few moments Diane came back out in her hospital scrubs. She told him what to do for dinner, not to watch too much TV. She looked at the sink and told him he was wasting water.

Claire turned off the faucet. "Don't forget to ask at work."

"Ask for what?"

"The day off," he said. "Friday. Remember, you're the next contestant on *The Price Is Right*."

Claire woke to shouting out on the street, Tammy's voice, pointed and accusatory. At his window he watched the lights coming on at the Bartletts' house, and listened to Tammy yelling, louder than normal, then Bruce yelling back, lower but no less angry, their shouts building to screeches that made Claire shake, standing with his face pressed against his Pufnstuf bed sheet.

The Bartletts' front door flew open and Claire saw Bruce cross the lawn. Tammy followed, still screaming, almost wordless now, just a primal high-pitched shriek, and then Bruce's voice, lower but just as loud and violent. He was dressed, but she was wearing a bathrobe that kept flying open, revealing her bra and pajama bottoms, the bare skin at her stomach. She followed

Bruce to the driveway, to his truck, and when he got inside she started pounding on the door, then the hood, still screaming as he started the engine. When he began to back the truck out, she moved as if to block it, but he shot an arm out his window and pushed her away. She stumbled sideways and he gunned the engine, backing out onto the street, and when she started to scream again, he put the truck in gear and drove up over the hedges lining the driveway and onto the lawn itself, full bore, cranking the wheel and turning doughnuts, digging up grass and flower beds, flinging cacti into the air. Tammy's screams matched the whine of the truck's engine. Lights came on up and down the street, other neighbors stepping out of their front doors in their own robes and pajamas, craning their necks to see. The truck spun in a whirl of plants and dirt, then beelined back out onto the street, pausing for one final scream from Tammy before tearing off down the road.

"What the hell?" Diane said. She stood in Claire's doorway in her nightgown. Claire didn't know how long she'd been watching. He turned back to his window. Tammy was up now, robe flapping, staggering across the ruined front lawn.

Diane went back to her bedroom. The neighbors went back inside their houses, leaving Claire to watch alone. The sound of the truck and the screaming still seemed to ring, filling the street. He could see Tammy standing in the middle of her yard. She lifted her arms, then dropped them to her sides. Her palms smacked against her thighs. After a moment, she knelt where a poppy bed had been and began gathering the uprooted flowers, trying without much success to set them back into their holes in the dirt.

The day of the taping, they ate breakfast in nervous silence. Diane was wearing the pale blue dress from her first date. She sat drinking coffee, asking Claire to call out products so she could name the price. Finally, Claire said, "You're ready. You gotta relax." Diane smiled and stood from the table, mussing his hair as she passed to the sink.

At school, Claire couldn't concentrate. He kept picturing Diane out in Television City, imagining what that place must be like. Some kind of radiant electronic kingdom—like Oz, maybe. Maybe Diane had been right.

At lunchtime, he walked out the front doors at school and rode home and turned on *The Price Is Right*, as if somehow he'd see her, as if the show weren't taped a week in advance. There was Bob Barker shepherding a giddy old man toward the Show-case Showdown. There was Anitra Ford in a flowing paisley-print dress revealing the price of an Amana refrigerator/freezer. A contestant guessed wrong about Spic and Span. Diane would have known that one. Diane would have gotten that one right.

When the show was over, he went into the bathroom, noticed the water level in the toilet was low. He flushed and the plumb-ing coughed, pushing back up into the bowl. There were little squares of paper floating on top now, torn neatly from larger sheets. It was Steve's note, what was left of it. Claire recognized the handwriting in the blurred ink.

He rode around the neighborhood, slowing down every time he passed the mess that was now the Bartletts' front yard, the clumps of sod and mud, the scattered piles of flowers and grass. The tire marks from Bruce's truck had hardened deep into the ground, like fossilized tracks from some prehistoric beast. Claire hadn't seen the truck since the night of the fight; hadn't seen Bruce at all. Every morning when he brought the newspaper up the driveway he snuck a peek in the garage windows, but Tammy's Fiat was the only car there.

Back in his room, he drew up that week's invoice and then walked across the street, up the long drive to the Bartletts' front door. Bruce had always answered when he'd knocked before, but this time, of course, it was Tammy. She was wearing the same purple robe she'd had on the night of the fight. She wasn't wearing any makeup, and her hair was a mess. It looked like she'd just gotten out of bed. Claire wanted to ask about Bruce, when Bruce would be back, *if* Bruce would be back, but now, facing her, he couldn't think of anything to say. He looked past her into the hallway. He'd never been inside their house. He had no idea what was in there, how big it was, how many rooms.

He stood on the smooth red porch where he'd once set his cheek and held out the invoice. Tammy flinched, like he had pointed a weapon. Then she took the invoice and looked it over and handed it back.

"I can get my own paper from now on," she said, and closed the door.

* * *

He was pulling listless wheelies in front of their house when the Corolla turned into the driveway. He pedaled up to the car, looking in the windows, at the back seat for any sign of cash and prizes. Diane got out, set her purse on the roof. She turned to Claire, shrugged her shoulders, clapped her hands at her sides. There was so much he wanted to ask, about Television City, about Bob Barker and Anitra Ford, about Johnny Olson, what his voice sounded like in person, booming in that big room. But something in her face, in her body, stopped him. Diane looked shaken, stunned. She looked so thin—he hadn't noticed how thin she'd become. Like a good wind, like one of those Santa Anas, could blow her off down the street.

"There were so many people there, waiting outside," she said. "You wouldn't believe all the people. But I had my VIP pass, so they took me right to the front of the line. You should have seen the looks people gave me. They brought us in for interviews with the producers, these very nice young men. We only had a few seconds. Some of the others were acting like idiots. Pick me, pick me. Desperate. I wouldn't do that. I tried to think about the questions. I wanted to give good answers, intelligent answers, but they were already moving us along again."

She shook her head, still smiling. "I sat there for the whole hour, waiting for my name. And, Claire, I knew all the prices! Every one! I kept waiting, thinking, *Call me, I know these things!*"

Her smile widened, trembling, then it gave altogether and Diane turned, picking up her purse and slamming it down again on the roof of the car. She started coughing, started yelling.

"This goddamned smoke! I can barely breathe!" She turned back to him. Her eyes were wet. She shook her head.

"I feel lied to," she said. "I feel like I lied to you."

She closed the door and carried her purse inside. Claire sat on his bike for a while, then rode it back out into the street, imagining the Bartlett twins' ramp there, the line of traffic backed up. He understood now why they'd done it, despite the risks, injuries and cops and punishment. He could imagine it, shutting everything down, making everything stop and be right for just a moment. Racing down the street, the suspended moment, their tires, his tires, hitting the end of the ramp and then lifting, weightless in air.

The day of the broadcast Claire skipped out of school again before lunch, even though the principal had called Diane about his last skip and Diane had warned him that the bike would go, TV privileges would go, if he ever did it again. He rode through the quiet neighborhood, the midday ghost town, everyone at school, at work. In their living room he stood and stared at the TV, wondering if he should turn it on, like if he watched the show there could be a different outcome, Johnny Olson would call Diane's name and she would throw her arms up and scream and *Come on down!* She would show them all what she knew, stunning Bob and Anitra, spinning the Big Wheel, nailing the Showcase Showdown. Instead, he stared at the dark screen for a while until he heard the sound of a truck engine outside. He turned to the window just in time to see the familiar blue pickup driving off down the street.

Claire opened the front door and found an envelope wedged under the security screen. Inside was that last week's invoice, in Bruce's handwriting, including everything Claire had done, even the leaf raking, and then another line down at the bottom, right above Bruce's signature. It read, *Severance, $5*, and then below that another line, *Buy a second brake for that bike*.

Claire took the puzzle box from the closet and brought it into his room. His window was open and there was a slight breeze blowing, the last gasp of the Santa Anas. The Pufnstuf bed sheet moved with it, revealing the view of the Bartletts' house, the mountains beyond. Claire pressed the box's hidden button in the sunflower petal and put his pay and the invoice in the bottom drawer.

He was outside on the bike when Diane got home. She climbed out of the car, brushing something from the front of her scrubs. "Crumbs," she said. "I had a late lunch."

He rode up the driveway with her and she put her lunch bag down on the front step and sat, blew out a breath. She looked at him sitting above her on the bike.

"I don't know where else to go," she said. "Is there anywhere else you want to go?"

Claire looked across the street to the Bartletts', the top of the tall oak reaching high above their roof, the mountains bathed in sundown. The late afternoon light was warm on his face and arms. He thought of Bruce standing under that tree, in this light, his arms raised, his eyes closed.

When Claire looked back, Diane was still watching him, waiting for an answer. He shook his head.

"No," he said. "Just here."

She nodded and looked past him, facing west, and he turned to see what she saw. Past the silhouettes of rooftops and telephone poles and TV antennas the sky deepened, the faded pickup blue going metallic purple and pink, shining in the smog, the distant palm trees standing tall against a cherry-red burst at the horizon.

"Well, look at that," Diane said. "My God, would you look at that."

Interstellar Space

When we were girls, we would lie in the cool blue orb of the above-ground pool in the backyard, our bodies flat across the surface, heads down, arms out, lifeless, what we called Dead Man's Float, five minutes, ten, lifting our chins only for quick gulps of air, then back down, eleven minutes, twelve, counting in our heads and waiting for our mother's voice from the kitchen window, calling, *Girls?*, then a pause, and in the waiting silence we could feel her watching, her straining concentration, squinting into the sun toward the pool, then calling again, this time with a small note of panic in her voice, a tight, electric trill, *Girls, are you all right?*, still holding our breath, cheeks full and lungs burning, listening for the sound of the screen door clacking shut, the frantic swish of our mother's bare feet running through the grass.

Girls!

We played Dead Man's Float; we played Prisoner. Meg curled on the floor of the aluminum shed, her wrists and ankles bound with silver duct tape stolen from our father's workbench.

A rough rag in her mouth, a blindfold. Tell me what you know. I paced the warped wooden floor, poking her ribs with my big toe. Pasadena summers in the mid-fifties; twenty years ago now. The interior of the shed hotter than hell. An Easy-Bake Oven, walls scalding to the touch. Both of us soaked in sweat, our skin reeking with chlorine. Tell me the truth this time. Meg thrashing and moaning or lying preternaturally still, her body going slack. Dead Man's Float out of water. Frustrated by Meg's will to silence, tired of asking questions, I'd release her and we'd switch places, the tape around my wrists and ankles now, the rags in my mouth, over my eyes. Meg pacing the shed, the whispered interrogation. My turn to withhold, to try not to break. But I was never as skilled a prisoner; I couldn't hold out nearly as long. I gave in to the ache in my arms and legs, the choking panic of the gag filling my mouth. I wasn't able to go inside like Meg did, the full withdrawal from questions, from the shed, the world. Occupying some distant interior space, there but not there, not really.

I sit on the bench by the window in the visiting room, waiting for Manuel, the orderly. The hospital was designed to resemble one of the classic Spanish missions dotting the California coastline. The floor is tiled terra-cotta red; the doorway is set within a high, smooth arch. The windows, though, are modern and institutional: thick glass shot through with wire mesh. Outside in the courtyard, the thinnest branches of the sycamores sway gently in the ocean breeze.

The door opens and Manuel comes through, holding Meg by the arm. Today's a bad day, I can see it in her face. She's gone in. The blank retreat. He leads her to the bench, waits for her to sit. He looks at me, nods. Meg moves away from him and sits at the other end of the bench. Manuel walks back to stand by the door.

Meg stares intently at the floor tiles. I smile, trying to draw her attention. I ask how she's doing. Manuel clears his throat, then raises his eyebrows in apology for the disturbance. He's young, maybe twenty, big and soft-faced, his hair slicked up and back from his high forehead. Once, on another bad day when Meg had folded completely within herself, he'd told me that he was in a punk band. They played down in L.A. sometimes, a couple of bars in Chinatown. I should come check them out, he'd said. I didn't hold the self-promotion against him. He was just trying to break the silence. How many meetings like this did he chaperone every day? I couldn't blame him for wanting to hear some semblance of normal conversation in the room.

I turn back to Meg, about to speak again, when the speakers up on the opposite wall begin to hum. A woman's voice follows, slightly muffled, paging one of the doctors. Meg's eyes widen. She lifts her face toward me, leans in.

"Do you hear that?"

A harsh whisper. She isn't talking about the announcement. The announcement is over. But whoever had spoken has forgotten to switch off the microphone, leaving a low electric hum in the room.

"Yes," I say.

"Those little voices."

"Yes."

This is how we've been instructed to respond, how we've been advised by her doctors. Try to agree, to normalize the situation. Of course I hear the voices, Meg. Everybody does.

"They're just little voices," I say. "Like kids playing. Just ignore it. I'm going to ignore it, too."

Manuel clears his throat again. I think maybe he's sending a signal, but when I look over he's staring down at the toes of his work boots, tapping one, then the other, pantomiming kicks to the pedals of a drum kit.

There's another click from above, the microphone channel finally cutting out, closing the room into silence. Meg lifts her head toward the speakers, but her eyes are still on mine. Scared now, almost pleading. I start to move closer on the bench but her face hardens quickly, shooting me a warning. She turns back toward the speaker, one ear cocked.

"That," she says, insistent, anguished. "Do you hear it?"

Meg started hearing things when she was ten. Voices, animal noises, a high-pitched tone that traveled in a stereophonic phase, one ear to the other. Through my brain, she told us. It's going through my brain.

Our parents took her to get her hearing checked. Everything was fine. Our pediatrician said it was probably an overactive imagination. Invisible friends. Give it time, he said. It will pass.

Back to the hearing specialists when she was eleven, when she was twelve. Nothing turned up. She had a hard time concentrating at school. Her grades suffered. We visited doctors up in Thousand Oaks, in Valencia, our father's colleagues at Caltech. They ran tests, asked questions. There was nothing physically wrong. It seemed no one wanted to discuss the alternative. Everyone bet on time. Give it time. Our house became a tense space, hours or days of normalcy always felt precarious, waiting for that silence from Meg that would upset the fragile equanimity we worked so hard to maintain. Everyone sitting for dinner at the kitchen table and Meg turning to the radio mounted under the cabinets, saying, *What?* Meg in her pinwheel dress, her thin body covered in multicolored spirals. KFAC on the radio, Mahler or Bartók or Holst's *Planets,* our father's favorite, strings and horns swelling but Meg hearing something else, standing from her chair and taking a step toward the speaker, her voice rising in accusation. *What did you say to me?*

And then it seemed to go away. She had just turned thirteen, and she stopped responding to these phantom callings. Our parents thought we were clear. It was only a phase. The doctors had been right.

But I knew. I spent the most time with her. Two grades ahead but in the same school. Seeing her in the hall talking to a friend and then stopping, right in the flow of kids moving this way and that. Meg stepping to the side, out of the stream, putting a hand to the wall to steady herself. Looking behind her, looking up. That helpless, fearful expression on her face. I saw it, but I said nothing. I was afraid of returning to that place of fear and uncertainty, the doctors' appointments, our parents' arguments. I didn't want her to drag us all back there, and so I kept silent, too.

In the desert, I walk the newly paved streets of the colonists' neighborhood, past earth-toned ranches and bungalows, 1950s Fords and Chevys in the driveways, wooden mailboxes standing at rigid attention, flags raised. This is what the future looks like, at least the movie-future: comforting and sentimental. In the script, settlers from Earth have colonized this barren planet, and the governing corporation built a mid-century American suburbia to help ease their shock on the alien world.

My designs are based on our old street in Pasadena. The neighbors' houses and cars, the corner market with the butcher's cleaver on the sign over the door. The main character and his wife live in our old house, a bark-brown bungalow with green shutters and a roll-back swing hanging on the porch. The house is empty inside, but parts of the interior have been dressed so that from certain angles, looking through the windows, it appears inhabited. That was our couch; those were our drapes. Through a bedroom window you can see the same knock-off Tiffany lamp I had when I was a girl in that room.

The only noticeable difference between the real and the re-created is that there's no pool in this backyard. When the movie begins, water still has to be shipped in from Earth. The plot then follows the construction of an enormous machine that will create the water necessary to colonize the rest of the planet. The machine is my design, too—a gleaming, monstrous, city block–sized cephalopod squatting in the desert, its pipes like tentacles reaching deep into the sand. The scale model sits in a soundstage on the lot in Culver City, waiting for its shots.

In the movie, they call the planet *Thalassa*, after a Greek sea spirit, as if the act of naming something can force it into being, making the thing conform to the name itself, the story they want to live within. Of course, it doesn't end well. None of these stories do. A religious cult sabotages the water machine and ends up flooding the planet. The final shot follows a single escape pod fleeing into space, the main character's wife and young son inside, the only survivors. As the frame fades, the camera pulls back to show Thalassa from an increasing distance, its red skin slowly drowning in blue.

Our shed is out there as well, in the back corner of the Astro-turfed yard. I don't know why I included it in the design, or why I insisted on its exact style and color. There aren't any scenes set back there. It might make its way into the blurred background of a shot staged in front of the house, or an overhead view of the colony, but it isn't a necessary component of the film.

Meg once told me that the first time she heard a voice was while we were playing Prisoner, as she lay taped and gagged on the floor of the shed. I was asking questions, demanding that she tell me her friends' secrets, where she hid things in her bedroom, when she heard a man speaking to her, just below the level of a normal conversational voice. She had to strain to hear. She tried to tell me to shut up so she could listen but the gag was in her mouth. She started thrashing on the floor, struggling to get free.

I remember that day. At first I thought she was playing, but then it was obvious something serious was happening. I untaped her, pulled the gag. She staggered to the wall, her back against the hot metal. I started to say something but she held up a hand for silence. She was listening, her face pinched with the effort. *What?* she said. *What?* I didn't know whom she was talking to. It looked like she was going to cry.

"Did you hear that?" she said, breathing hard, like she'd just run a race. "What did he say?"

We never set foot in there again. For the rest of our childhood, through all the tests and doctor visits, neither of us said another word about the shed. We ignored it like an unwanted or embarrassing relation. A silent, scary uncle who sits brooding at the far end of the dinner table. Don't look at him; don't catch his attention.

When I was sketching the initial designs for the film, the shed was the first thing that I drew. It was there on the page, suddenly, forming under the tip of my pencil. Reemerged. For whatever reason, I found that I couldn't go any further with the rest of the design until I had its likeness just right. The shed came first and everything else followed.

Out in our reconstructed backyard, I tap a finger on the aluminum doors, listen to the familiar hollow metal pang. I know it sounds crazy, but sometimes I wonder what would have happened if our roles had been reversed that day, when Meg heard the first voice. If I had been on the ground, restrained, helpless, and she had been standing above. If I would have heard it instead, as if it were an objective event, a lightning strike, and that's all that would have mattered, who was where in that moment.

When *Explorer 1* launched from Cape Canaveral, our mother threw a party in the backyard. Our father had helped design the rocket carrying the satellite, which was sent up to detect cosmic rays. If all went well, the satellite would stay in orbit for just over a hundred days, sending data back to Earth until its batteries ran dry.

It was January, a few weeks after Meg heard that first voice in the shed. The night of the launch, our back lawn was a checkerboard of picnic blankets, our neighbors and some of our father's colleagues reclining, looking skyward while our father grilled burgers and our mother stepped unsteadily between bodies, pouring drinks. Meg and I staked our blanket at the far end of the yard, right by the shed. Our father had given us a star map and binoculars, had unstrapped his wristwatch so we could keep track of the time change from Florida. Meg was far more interested than I in the astronomical component of the gathering. I'd just turned twelve, and spent most of the night in the corner by the fence, whispering with my friends about the neighborhood boys in attendance.

Finally, about an hour after sunset, Meg stood from our blanket and announced that it was time. Our mother went inside the house and shut off all the lights. Kids smothered flashlight beams.

We all lay back on our blankets, passing binoculars, looking up into the darkness. I could hear whispers from some of the kids, murmurs and giggling from some of the adults. Meg shushed everyone, as if the lack of light required an absence of sound as well, an absolute stillness in which to see. After a number of false sightings, she finally pointed out a tiny orange glow climbing through the field of stars. There, she said, that's it. Silence again, until one of the men from the other side of the yard said in hushed, almost solemn confirmation: It could be. We all sat quietly then, watching until the orange light disappeared.

Later, long after our parents had gone to bed, I was awakened by a sound from Meg's bedroom. I stood looking through the doorway across the hall to where she sat on her bed, her flashlight beam pointed down at the star chart unfolded across her sheets. Her finger traced the rising arc we'd followed a few hours before. Her face, though, was no longer full of the wonder I'd seen earlier in the backyard, but was now tightened with anxiety. She followed the rocket's route over and over, her expression shifting from tension to horror, as if she was confirming something beyond belief, the explanation of a great and awful truth. I thought of asking her what was wrong, but I didn't. I was tired and foggy with sleep. I don't remember going back to bed, but I must have, leaving Meg alone and awake in the night.

By her fourteenth birthday, it had become obvious that Meg really hadn't gotten any better. She started talking back to the radio again, arguing with the TV. She used her allowance to buy a jar of foam earplugs from the hardware store on Green Street, little bright orange buds she'd seen on construction workers, men paving the freeways. She wore them everywhere. People thought she was deaf. The four of us would go out to dinner on Friday nights, and the teenage hostess at the front counter would see the neon blobs in Meg's ears and smile uncomfortably, self-conscious in the presence of the handicapped. Once, an old man at the library came up and started gesturing in sign language, delighted to find another who might understand, but Meg grabbed me when she saw his fluttering hands, her grip tight on my blouse, pulling me back toward the doors, as if he was some kind of dark magician casting a spell.

"Don't you know what he's doing up there?"

Sometimes I'd wake to Meg's whispers in the night. Turning on the Tiffany lamp, I'd find her on her hands and knees beside my bed, having crawled in from her own room.

"Dad and those men," Meg would hiss at me, "shooting those things into space?"

Not long after she'd begun hearing voices and noises, she'd decided that our father was responsible. She'd drawn a line from his rockets to the things she heard. In Meg's mind, one came directly from the other.

"Go away!" I'd whisper back. "Go back to bed!"

My concern for Meg was starting to be overshadowed by the disgust I felt at her accusations about our father. I didn't want to hear her ramblings about him, the insinuation that she understood something that my mother and I refused to acknowledge.

Kneeling beside my bed, she'd pull at my covers, trying to drag me down with her.

"They can find us anywhere from up there."

"Mom!" I would call. "Dad!"

"Cate, please!" Her fingers clutching my sheets as the hall light snapped on and our parents came through the door. "Don't you know what they're doing?"

It was back to the doctors, the hearing specialists; finally, a psychiatrist. Things seemed to stabilize for a while, but Meg took a turn when she started high school. She began forcing herself to throw up, trying to purge microwaved impurities from her body. She found the same roll of duct tape we'd used to play Prisoner and wrapped long lengths around her head, covering her ears. Hair and skin came away when our mother pulled it loose.

Then one afternoon the summer before her sophomore year, we got a call from the police. They'd picked her up over on Lake Avenue, handing out mimeographed flyers to rich ladies trying to shop.

Hello my name is Margaret Rose Yates and I have been bombarded with signals and instructions since I was a child. These are direct attacks on my brain and thoughts. My father works with the Jet Propulsion Laboratory and this is where

the signals originate. I am very sorry to interrupt your day
but I am asking for your help.

Her psychiatrist called our parents to his office. Meg and I stayed home. I was packing for my upcoming summer job as a camp counselor up in Big Bear. I poked through my closet, deciding which clothes to take along, while Meg packed some things in her room, ready to move into mine, as she always did while I was away. She seemed fine again that afternoon. Back then it still happened that way—Meg switched quickly from a girl who passed out flyers on Lake Avenue to one who chatted with me from across the hall. I tried to convince myself that things would be okay, that she would now settle back into this version of herself. The summer would pass uneventfully, and the next year I would move away to college. Meg would finish high school and come to live with me out in Chicago or New York, wherever I had begun my adult life, and we'd get an apartment in the new city, a place of our own where we'd talk like this again, back and forth through our open doorways.

We heard the car pull into the driveway. I looked out my window and saw our parents coming toward the house. Mom had been crying. Dad looked stunned, weak and lost, as if all certainty had been sucked from his body. I heard Meg call from the other room. She was at her window, too. "*No!*" she shouted. I thought she was shouting at them, but then I realized she was shouting to me.

"Keep them away from me! Don't you see, Cate? Here they come! Keep them away!"

* * *

There's a bench by a fig tree in the hospital courtyard, where I sit with Meg on her good days, and where I sit alone on her bad. Today is a good day, so I tell Meg about the movie I'm working on. I show her designs, sketches, and watercolors. That's our house, she says. That's the Robinsons', the Robecks'. That's Dad getting into his blue Customline in his matching blue suit.

She asks me for the movie's story, and so I tell her about the settlers and the water machine, the cult, the flood. About the single escape pod rocketing back toward Earth. She nods, listening, her eyes closed again.

I watch her face, seemingly at peace. I sit back on the bench and close my own eyes, careful, trying to share the borders of Meg's rest. I want to tell her another story, in the hope that the act of telling could make it true. Two girls, sisters, play Dead Man's Float, play Prisoner. I could show you drawings, Meg. I could show you watercolors, photographs from the set. The girls play in the shed in their backyard and when they're finished or hungry or their mother calls out to them, they reemerge into the sunlight, hand-in-hand, unchanged.

After the flyers, Meg wasn't even allowed to finish the school year. My parents drove her up to the hospital, where they were told she'd only need to spend the summer. This became a repeated refrain, season by season. She'll only need to spend the fall, the winter. Eventually, the doctors stopped promising, and we stopped expecting a return.

Right after Meg went away, just before the end of the school year, a boy named Donnie Rush stopped me on the way to Calculus. Donnie was an awkward, overgrown boy, a friend of Meg's. I tried to push past him, afraid of what he might say. Our official story was that Meg had gone to live with our aunt in Vermont, to study art at a special high school there. But the truth had begun to seep out. Whispers in the school halls, in the aisles of the drugstore, the corner market.

Donnie continued to block my path, and finally steered me into a classroom doorway. He wanted to show me what he had under his jacket. It was one of Meg's flyers. He said he'd found it stapled to a telephone pole on Lake Avenue, while he was shopping with his mother. I grabbed it from him, and he looked offended, backing away to the row of lockers. I brought it here to give it to you, he said. I didn't want someone else to see it up on that pole.

I went straight to the bathroom, locked myself in a stall and flushed the flyer down the toilet. Pushing the handle again and again to make sure it was gone. The bell rang out in the hallway for the start of the new period, but I stayed in the stall with the water whooshing down through the toilet, as if with each flush I could push it farther away.

We all visit separately now: Mom, Dad, me. Our parents divorced a year after Meg was admitted. Looking back, it's possible to believe that the tension she created in the house was what held them together. Without it, a line had been cut, finally freeing them to fall in opposite directions.

There were years when Meg wouldn't come out to the visiting room if our father was present. That seems to have passed. He describes her now as resigned toward seeing him. They don't talk much. He brings her books, poetry mostly. He has an idea of poetry as beautiful and harmless. Long-form greeting cards. A few times I've had to call and tell him that Sylvia Plath and John Berryman may not be the best gift-giving ideas.

Once he called me near tears. I'd never seen or heard our father cry, but he had just come back from a visit where he'd told Meg that he'd retired, that he no longer had anything to do with the lab, with rockets and satellites. He said he didn't know where the impulse had come from, he'd just said it, and that she'd looked at him with such heartbreaking relief that he'd had to admit it was a lie.

It's impossible not to make things worse, he'd told me on the phone that night.

Another year passed before Meg would see him again.

A couple of months ago, I got a phone call from Donnie Rush. I hadn't seen him since high school. He was living up in Thousand Oaks, he said. Married, two kids, girls, three years apart. He'd gotten my number from another old classmate I was still in contact with. He said he hoped he wasn't intruding.

He asked if I thought it would be okay if he went to visit Meg. He thought about her a lot, he said, wondered how she was. He'd had a crush on her back in school, even after he'd found the flyer, though the flyer had scared him. She was so beautiful, so smart, he said. And then she was gone.

She would have been a great beauty. Our mother often tells me this after many gin and tonics at one of our dinner dates in Santa Monica or Malibu, seafood with an ocean view, walls of glass on the water. I always snap back, defending Meg, as if this is a frivolous observation, malicious even. Mom, really, you're being unkind. But she's right. There was an undeniable beauty there, the full waves of sandy hair and those eyes, deep reddish brown, the color of good, rich earth. It was a beauty almost from another time, something close to nature. But it had all been shadowed by the fear that starved her face to skin and bone, that drove her to pull handfuls of hair out by the roots.

What do you expect, Mom? I say, staring back through the windows at the waves lashing the beach. How should she look? She's afraid all the time.

I told Donnie that he was welcome to visit, that it might be good for Meg to see an old friend. I had to stop myself from sounding like our mother, telling him to temper his expectations, the picture he had of her from twenty years ago.

She has good days and bad, I said, and he told me he'd keep that in mind.

In a production meeting out at the location, the director tells me they're going to tear down the shed. It's in the way of a shot, and has no real use in the film. I argue to keep it, surprising myself with my vehemence, nearly shouting at him across the conference tent. When he gives in, I go back out to our reconstructed yard and stand in the space where the pool would be, looking at the shed. I know why I wanted it here. Maybe I always knew. Building the shed was an act of narrative erasure, like flushing Meg's flyer down the school toilet. Even when I first sketched it, I could imagine sitting in a theater with the finished film, waiting for the final shots after the water machine explodes and watching the planet, the neighborhood, the yard, the shed, flooded, splintered, swept away.

Donnie Rush called again after his visit. Before he saw Meg, one of the nurses had given him the usual instructions, to keep his voice low, to agree with whatever Meg said. And so he had, sitting on a bench in the visiting room, corroborating for Meg that there were voices coming from the PA speakers, electrostatic waves shooting down from passing planes. He said this seemed to calm her, but that then there was nothing left, they just sat there in the shared fiction.

"What more did you want?" I said.

"I just wanted her to talk," he said. His voice was so much deeper than I remembered, a man's voice, a father's voice.

"I always found Meg so interesting," he said. "I just wanted her to talk so I could listen."

Our mother doesn't use the term. The diagnosis. She doesn't think it's helpful. She's worried, I think, that it has some talismanic power, that saying it aloud will make it truer than it already is.

We're sitting at another table by the windows. Mom's into her second G & T and I'm staring out down to the beach, the rolling purple dark. She's talking about Meg's missed opportunities, all the things she could have done, could have been, a teary litany, if only this curse hadn't befallen, the evil spell, the mental weakness, whatever it might be in all its mystery. Suddenly I'm standing, I find myself on my feet, though no one else in the restaurant is looking, not even Mom. Her eyes are fixed on the rim of her glass and I shout it, the term, the diagnosis, as loud as I can. It sounds like I'm making an announcement, calling out a door prize, someone's a winner, and now there's silence in the dining room and all eyes are on me, even Mom's, heads turned and chins raised. The words in the room now. Who wants to claim them, who wants to reach up and take hold?

It's a bad day, so we're in the visiting room, on the bench by the windows. Meg looks like she hasn't slept in a week, her face haggard and terror-struck.

I'm talking about the movie, a couple of new scenes the screenwriters have added, watching Meg's expression as I babble. I tell her that it turns out we might build the pool after all, that the writers now want a scene where the kids stand out in the arid heat and stare longingly at its empty shell.

There's no change in her face, so I push on, talking about our pool now, our real pool, filled with cool water on a summer afternoon. Remember Dead Man's Float, Meg? Remember that feeling? The held breath, the silence underwater, like time had stopped all around us. Then Mom's panicked voice pulling us back to the world of light and air.

Come up, I want to say, reaching across the bench. Meg, come back. It should be so easy to come back. But she flinches at my touch, regathering herself in. My hand drops to the wooden seat.

There's no cure for any of this. No mother's call, no alien planet fantasy, no retelling of a childhood story that will change things. There's no explanation, no logic. Two sisters in a yard on a summer afternoon. Only one will ever leave that place. Only one will make it safely away.

There's a crackle of static from the speakers up on the wall, an electronic throat clearing, then a woman's voice paging a doctor. Her voice ends, but she's left the channel open and now there's a low buzz coming through, like the drone of an insistent bee. Meg's eyes broaden, bringing some life to her face.

"Do you hear that?" she says, looking toward the speaker.

I think about all the visits, all the hours in this room. Our mother, our father, Donnie Rush. Everyone sitting, as Donnie said, in the shared fiction.

"Cate." Meg turns to me, her eyes on mine, desperate. "Do you hear that?"

"No," I say. "I don't. Tell me about it."

In the Red

The traffic cop didn't see things my way. The night Deb left I got pulled over, driving to I don't know where. Around. The cop made me get out of my car, empty my pockets. He saw the roll of quarters I always keep, asked me what they were for. Laundry, I said. The cop asked if I'd been drinking. I said that I had. He said, Where were you drinking? and I said I'd bought a six-pack at the junior market and had sat right down in the parking lot. He said, Aren't you a little old to be drinking in parking lots? and I said, Aren't you a little old to have that stupid fucking mustache, and so here I am.

There are enough guys in the cafeteria to fill two long tables. Some rough-looking characters. Even the chubby accountants— the middle managers or whatever, guys in suits and ties—even they have a threatening edge. They don't have to smile in their office or cheer at their son's ball game or be anything but what they really are. This is reality in here. This is no bullshit.

A couple guys know each other from previous classes. Nods and handshakes. Long time no see.

Our instructor walks into the cafeteria. She's in her forties, I'd guess, a short woman with frizzy hair, big glasses, wearing a dark blue pantsuit. She says her name is Connie, thanks us all for being on time, crosses to a small table at the front of the room. She's carrying a large purse and a larger book bag, and when she gets to the table she lets each of them slide off her shoulders. While her back is turned, one of the guys whistles— a long, low wolf whistle—and Connie turns and gives him a look because she knows she's not the kind of woman who gets a whistle like that. Her look says, If you're going to be a fucking asshole then be a fucking asshole but don't pretend you want me up on this table, legs in the air. Let's not make this about something it's not.

The guy nods, lowers his eyes. His name is Luis—we'd already introduced ourselves. He's the youngest guy in the class, seems like a real smartass, with a nasty scar cutting down through his mouth and black teardrop tattoos up at the corner of each eye. He keeps his eyes down, nodding; such is the fierceness of Connie's look. Okay. Understood.

Connie says, Somebody's got to wheel in the chalkboard from out in the hall.

A couple of guys go out and come back in pushing the chalkboard.

Where you want it?

Right here is fine, Connie says. Just turn it so everybody can see.

She pulls a couple of books out of her bag, a couple of folders, a fistful of pens tied with a rubber band. She takes off her watch and sets it face-up on the table.

You'd better go get your coffee and pop and M&M's now, she says, because we don't do the break at 8:30.

There's always a break at 8:30.

Not here.

It's the law.

Not here.

Everybody goes out in the hall to the vending machines, gets their coffee and sodas and candy. Rolled eyes, clucked tongues. Can you believe this bitch? What happened to the other guy, Doug, the guy who did class last time? Doug was a good guy.

Back in the cafeteria, metal chairs squeaking, soda can tabs popping, wrappers tearing. Connie waits for the noise to finish.

Okay, she says. Who can tell me why we're here?

To learn to deal with our hostile emotions in a safe and responsible manner. A lumbering chorus of voices, a follow-up snickering wave.

Good to see we have some veterans in the class, Connie says. Yes. To learn to deal with our hostile emotions in a safe and responsible manner. Connie writes this on the board.

The middle-manager type sitting behind Luis clears his throat. And how do we go about doing that, he says.

Connie turns. What's that?

You're supposed to ask us how we go about dealing with our hostile emotions in a safe and responsible manner.

Connie turns back to the board. If you knew the answer to that, she says, you wouldn't be sitting here.

* * *

After class, a group heads to the parking lot while another group of us heads down to the corner to wait for the bus.

Luis is walking at the back, kind of dragging one leg, trying out a tough-guy limp. After a few drag steps, he calls out to the middle manager guy.

Who you got?

The middle manager guy turns, still walking. What are you talking about?

I'm talking about who breaks first, Luis says. Every class there's a couple guys who lose it, get popped, maybe put away for a while.

The middle manager guy thinks for a second, nods across the group to a tall dude with a ponytail. Him.

Fabio? Luis says. Nah, man, Fabio's a lover, not a fighter.

That's my pick, the middle manager guy says.

Fabio calls back from the front. I got Luis. Luis has been here, like, fifteen times.

Luis cackles, slaps his hand against his thigh.

We keep walking. I can see a few cars double-parked by the bus stop. Mothers, girlfriends, babies in car seats. Rides home.

How about you? Fabio says.

Luis drags his limp, moving through the group, looking. He finally settles on me. I got this big fucker, he says. He throws a crooked-toothed smile back at the group. This big fucker looks about ready to blow.

* * *

When I was a kid, my grandma called it Getting in the Red. She got the phrase from a TV commercial where this dumbass hadn't changed his oil for fifteen years or something and burns out his engine. They show the engine glowing like a hot coal, cycling faster and faster until it sputters and smokes out. *Stop your engine before it gets in the red*, the commercial announcer said.

Some kid out on the street or somewhere would call me Jonas the Whale or Jonas the Giant and I'd get so worked up that I'd start to shake and spit and just want to kill him for saying that.

Jonas! Grandma yelling, running down the lawn, apron and hands flapping. Jonas, you're getting in the red!

She'd pull me off the little fucker and drag me inside and I'd have to sit with my head on the kitchen table and a cold washcloth on the back of my neck. As soon as I felt that washcloth I'd start crying like a baby. The anger sucked out through my skin, into the cold wet cloth. My eyes closed, I could hear Grandma moving around the kitchen. Cooking sounds, dishwashing sounds, pots and pans clattering in the sink. Every few minutes she'd come over and change the water in the washcloth or just stand with her hand on the back of my neck while I choked through the end of my crying jag.

Jonas, you get so overwhelmed, she'd say. Jonas will you ever not be like this.

Maybe, Grandma, I'd say, sniffling snot, wiping my eyes. Maybe. I'll try.

Jonas, Grandma saying, you get so overwhelmed I don't know what to do.

This is a different life now. This is a waiting life. This is a life of standing through the day, legs aching, back aching, dragging items across the scanner, giving change, reading the customers' Rewards Club savings from their receipts. You saved four dollars and thirty-eight cents. Would you like help out to your car. Ricardo here will help. Thank you. Come again.

This is a different life now, since Deb left.

The house is mine, technically. My name is on the lease. A tiny two-bedroom place with security bars on the doors and windows; a jagged, waist-high fence around the mangy front yard. Not one of your better neighborhoods. I rented it because I could afford it and because it had a rickety old front porch. Grandma always said there was no point in living in a place without a front porch.

The afternoon Deb moved in she said, You've lived here for five years and still haven't bought curtains? It never crossed my mind to buy curtains, I said. Who cares about curtains. The next day there were blue curtains on all the windows. The day after that there was a toothbrush holder on the bathroom sink. When there's more than one toothbrush you need a toothbrush holder. What have you done to my house? I said. Deb pulled a new shower curtain from her shopping bag, started hanging it around the tub. I made it habitable, she said.

We always kept the TV on the kitchen counter. A little 13-inch job Deb bought with her employee discount at the department store. She liked to watch it while she cooked. I never had any goddamned use for the thing, except when the Cowboys were on, and then I'd have to pull a folding chair right up next to the screen to watch. Deb would say, Why don't we get a bigger TV so you won't go blind sitting so close to that thing? and I'd say that we didn't need a bigger TV because I didn't have any use for the thing except for every Sunday when the Cowboys were on. Not counting the playoffs. Or the Super Bowl. Then Deb would laugh at me and after a moment I'd laugh at me, too.

I've moved the TV out into the living room. The kitchen is not the best place to be right now because of this little chip in the Formica at the edge of the countertop. I keep telling myself that the chip has always been there, or that it's from Deb dropping a pickle jar or something, but I know how it really got there, what hit against the countertop hard enough to chip the Formica. So I carried the TV into the living room, which is where it belonged in the first place.

I've started watching the home shopping channel. I guess it reminds me of my grandma because she always used to watch it those last few months in the rest home. Also, it's the only thing on when I get out of work at three in the morning. Used to be that I would get home and have a few beers out on the front porch and watch the traffic go by on the freeway, and then I'd get in bed and just lie next to Deb until I fell asleep. But now Deb's gone and I can't sleep and so hence the home shopping channel.

There's this guy, Brian Lang, who's always on when I get home, this nerdy-looking guy with a kid's bowl cut and glasses.

He hosts the *Collectors' Corner* where they sell all types of Star Wars spaceship models and *Land of the Lost* painted plates and shit like that, all numbered and authenticated limited edition stuff. Two hundred bucks for a plate. He takes phone calls while he's showing the stuff and people talk about how much they love this plate or that comic book and when's he going to have some of those commemorative coins on the show. He really knows his stuff, all the details and facts and trivia. I might think this shit is stupid and maybe he does, too, but you'd never know it from watching him. He can talk about this stuff for hours, make it seem like he cares. People call and love talking to him because here's this normal guy with a job on TV who knows as much as they do about *Farscape* or whatever.

Tonight he's selling trading cards from some old space movie. Brian's into these cards because they're from thirty years ago and really hard to find. This kind of history is disappearing, he says. But the producers of the shopping channel found a whole case of them at an estate sale in Calabasas, still in their packages of six cards with a piece of bubble gum, although Brian says he wouldn't recommend trying the gum.

People are really going apeshit over these cards. All the usual losers are calling up, the people who call a couple times a week. They can't believe he found these cards. One guy yells into the phone, Thank you, Calabasas!

I play a drinking game while I watch. I drink a beer every time somebody says they've been waiting all night for these cards. I drink a beer every time somebody says they feel blessed.

It's getting boring, though; the game is too easy tonight, everybody is so worked up, so I decide to up the ante. If I get up to ten beers, I'm going to get on the phone and see what this idiot has to say for himself.

I feel so blessed, a caller says. I've been waiting for these cards all night.

Nine beers. Ten.

We have Jonas on the line from Los Angeles, Brian says. He looks into the camera. Are you there, Jonas?

I'm here.

You got on right in time, my friend. We're nearly out of cards.

My lucky night.

Are you a movie buff, Jonas?

No.

But you're a collector. You're a card collector.

No. I'm not a sucker, either.

On TV, Brian's smile freezes a little, the corners of his mouth tensing.

I'm glad to hear that, he says.

Fifty bucks for a pack of trading cards.

He's still smiling, but it's harder, tighter. These are highly collectible, he says, yes.

You're smarter than you look, Brian. All these dummies calling up to give you money.

I don't see it that way at all, Jonas.

Sure. You're really excited about these cards. I can tell.

You think I'm acting.

You said it, not me.

He's stopped smiling, but he hasn't hung up, or motioned for someone to cut me off.

Well, I don't know how to convince you, Jonas, he says. I think you either get it or you don't.

You don't think I get it?

It doesn't appear that way.

If I buy a pack of cards for fifty bucks will I get it?

If you buy a pack of cards for fifty bucks, he says, and you don't get it, you can send them back, no questions asked. Even if they're opened. Even if you've eaten the gum. He smiles again, looser now, confident. My personal guarantee.

I sit looking at the TV, Brian smiling at me in the living room. The phone's cradled between my ear and my neck. Your personal guarantee, I say.

Yes, sir.

Eleven beers.

Okay, I say. Send me one. I want to get it.

Nobody's technically in the Tuesday night class for hitting his wife or girlfriend. Technically, everybody's here for something else. If you get arrested for hitting your wife or girlfriend they don't send you to this group, they send you to another one, over at the courthouse. Or they send you to jail. This group is for if you got into a fight at a Dodgers game or pushed somebody at work or mouthed off to a cop who pulled you over. If you've got a history of these things. It's not supposed to be as serious as the group at the courthouse, but everybody still knows, everyone's still done it at some point. We know; Connie knows. Wife beaters. Woman hitters. It's like a smell in the room.

Tonight, Connie says, I'd like to talk about triggers.

We all sit in the same seats in the cafeteria. Connie hasn't told us we have to, but we do anyway. I sit halfway down the table on the right side, between Fabio and the Traffic Guy from Channel Four. Everybody was real impressed when the Traffic Guy showed up. They wanted his autograph, wanted to shake his hand. They wanted to know what it was like to pilot a helicopter. I'm not a pilot, he said, I just sit in the passenger seat and talk. He may not be a pilot, but he has the look of one, or the movie version of one, a commanding officer, brush-cut, block-jawed, and intense. He was embarrassed to be here and wanted to make sure no one was going to tell anybody. The guys all laughed because who the fuck are we going to tell? We all work late on Tuesday nights. This is what we tell people. We're all at the gym, at a poker game.

Every action has a trigger, Connie says. She writes this on the board: *Trigger. Action.* She draws a line connecting the two. What we need to do, she says, is break the connection between the Trigger and the Action. She wipes out a section of the line with a corner of the eraser. We need to start recognizing the things that make us angry and stop responding physically. Once we do that, she says, we can get to the root of the problem.

Give me some things, she says, that make you angry.

My boss, Luis says.

Connie writes it on the board. *Boss.*

What about your boss? she says.

He's an asshole.

What about him specifically?

He's a fucking asshole.

Things he does that make you angry.

Luis thinks. My boss got this look, he says. Like he doesn't want to be working there. Like he's better than that. And how's that supposed to make us feel, if he doesn't want to be working there and he's the boss?

Inferiority, Connie says.

How's that?

He makes you feel inferior. Makes you feel like you're wasting your time at that job.

Yeah, like how the fuck are we supposed to feel?

Connie writes *Inferiority* on the board across from *Boss* and draws a line connecting the two.

Who else has something?

The middle manager guy raises a finger. My neighbor, he says. Diagonal from my house.

And what does he do?

What does *she* do. She doesn't do anything. She walks down her driveway in the morning. Gets in her car. I sit at the kitchen window and drink my coffee.

And how does that make you angry?

She's so much hotter than my wife.

Connie writes *Disappointment* on the board. Draws a line to *Anger*.

Who else? she says.

Traffic, the Traffic Guy says.

Everybody laughs.

I'm serious, the Traffic Guy says. He looks serious. The stupidity of it, he says. People making the same mistakes every single day.

Connie writes *Traffic*, draws a line.

My dick's too big, says a guy in the back. My girlfriend keeps complaining that it hurts.

Everybody laughs. Connie writes *Delusions of Grandeur* on the board.

So we see, she says, that the nature of the Trigger isn't really important. Anything can set us off. What's important is recognizing the emotion caused by the Trigger and taking the time to figure an appropriate response. Not just jumping from *Inferiority* or *Disappointment* or *Traffic* straight to *Anger* straight to *Violence*. The important thing is not to get ahead of ourselves.

We've all had to buy notebooks for the class, just regular old spiral jobs from the supermarket school-supply aisle. I got mine thirty percent off. Employee perk. Some of the guys are writing things down in their notebooks, some are doodling. Some of the guys are ignoring their notebooks and ignoring Connie and staring out the cafeteria windows, even though it's almost ten o'clock and pitch black out. My notebook's blank.

Connie says, This week I want you to keep your notebooks with you at all times, and when something sets you off, write it down. Write it down and then write a one-line explanation, just one sentence, about why it's setting you off.

While it's happening, Luis says.

While it's happening, Connie says. Is that doable?

Sure, sure, it's doable.

Connie looks down at her watch on the table. We've got fifteen minutes left, she says.

The middle manager guy raises a finger. Can we go early?

No, Connie says. You can't.

Lots of grumbling in the cafeteria.

That sucks, the middle manager guy says.

Connie pulls up a chair, sits. Put it in your notebook, she says.

I see it, I see it, she says, this flat-faced, big-boned woman in line at the checkout, smiling wide. Not many people in the store. One thirty, quarter of two in the morning. My checkout's the only one open.

I see it, I see it, she says, pointing toward the dark windows at the front of the store, then up toward the ceiling, and then she falls flat on her back and starts to shake and froth at the mouth.

Holy shit, Ricardo shouts and drops his mop and runs the rest of the way down the cereal aisle to my checkout.

The woman fell on the guy behind her, this little hairy guy with a perm and a greasy face. She's lying on top of him with her eyes rolled up into her head, frothing and shaking, and he's trying to crawl out from under her.

Get her off me get her off me, he says.

I come around the checkout to where they're tangled in a heap. Ricardo's at the checkout now too and he says, She's having a seizure, Jonas—we got to hold her steady, so I kneel down and grab on to her shoulders.

The guy with the perm is struggling and yelling, Get her off me get her off me.

Shut up, don't move, I say to the guy, but he keeps struggling, trying to push the woman off him.

Fucking stop moving, I say.

Somebody get some juice, Ricardo says. Nobody in the store moves so Ricardo yells, Somebody get some juice, please, and this time the *please* is pained and sharp and this chick over in produce with a bunch of tattoos drops her shopping basket and runs toward the beverage cases.

I'm yelling at the perm guy, Fucking stop moving, because the woman is starting to choke on her froth and my hands are so sweaty I can't get a good grip on her shoulders.

Ricardo says, Jonas hold her steady.

I can't I fucking can't.

Help me get her mouth open, Ricardo says. Clear away some of that spit.

Shit shit shit, I'm saying.

Get her off me get her off me.

Jonas, open her mouth, Ricardo yells. Just keep her steady and open it.

Fucking stop moving, I scream at the perm guy, but he keeps pushing at the woman so I grab him by the shoulders and pull him out, across the floor to the front of the checkout, but he's still saying, Get Off Get Off, so I kneel down and put a hand over his mouth and slap him on the side of the head, slap him again, and now he's yelling and Ricardo's yelling and the tattooed chick's yelling and I'm punching this guy in the temples and now Ricardo's on top of me, pulling me away, and the tattooed chick is screaming, That woman! That woman! and Ricardo gives me another shove and stumbles back to the woman who's now thrashing on the floor. The tattooed chick hands Ricardo a carton of orange juice and he tears open the top and pours a little down the woman's throat. He pulls her head up on his knee and some of the juice spills out so Ricardo starts massaging her throat saying, Come on baby, come on baby please, let's get this down, let's get this down baby, and finally some of it goes down, finally she swallows. Shaking less and less. Just little jerks now, her head one way, her body the other. Her face is white and shiny, covered with sweat and juice.

I get to my feet and just stand there, watching. The perm guy is still lying on the floor, crying now, his arms folded over his face.

Jesus Christ, Ricardo says.

The ambulance comes. The paramedics rush in, radios squawking.

Deb's stuff is still here. Every night I get home from work and expect it all to be moved out. She has a key. But every night it's still here.

I imagine she's staying at her parents' house out in Riverside. I don't know where else she'd go. Probably getting an earful from her dad. Deb's mom was always really nice when I was over at their place for dinner or whatnot, but her dad never cared for me. After my first DUI he told Deb that how she lived her life was her business, but he didn't want me in their home anymore. So it was a really big deal when they invited me to dinner this last Thanksgiving. I can only imagine the shit Deb had to wade through. I told her that I was perfectly fine eating frozen pot pie at home and squinting at the Cowboys game in the kitchen, but she said it was all settled. There was going to be a truce between me and her dad. I said that there couldn't be a truce because we weren't fighting in the first place, that I honestly couldn't care less what the old fucker thought of me. Deb put her hand on the back of my neck, fingertips light at my hairline, whispering, *shhhh* into my ear until I unclenched my fists and teeth.

Deb's dad's a high school principal. He makes good money, I guess. Their neighborhood looks right out of a TV commercial: tree-lined street, SUVs in the driveways, lawns like putting greens. No one talked much during dinner. Deb kept asking her dad and me questions, trying to get the conversation started. We both answered in one word or less. Her mom served sparkling apple juice instead of wine. I could tell her dad was jonesing for a drink but wouldn't break down and have one in front of me after he'd said that shit about the DUI. I kept watching him, his hands shaking a little whenever he lifted his glass.

After dinner, Deb and her mom cleared the dishes, started

futzing in the kitchen. Her dad went into the living room and turned on the Cowboys game. I sat at the table alone for a few minutes, then I thought, What the hell, I don't want to miss the game. We sat on opposite ends of the couch. Every once in a while he'd say something about one of the players, what kind of season they were having, and then I'd say something and after a while I started to think, Well, this guy might be a blowhard but at least he knows a little about football.

Deb suggested we all play charades. Some kind of Thanksgiving tradition. And now, she said, wasn't it great because there were enough players for actual teams. It was Deb and her mom on one team, me and Deb's dad on the other. Deb's mom told her dad that he should turn off the game while we were playing, but he said, Let's leave it on for Jonas, which I thought was an all right thing to say.

It came down to the last round, Deb's dad stumbling around the living room, squinting, pawing the air in front of him, and when I guessed *Mr. Magoo* to win the game he was so excited he grabbed me around the shoulders with one arm and thumped me on the chest, laughing and shouting. This man knows how to play charades, he said, and I put my hands on his shoulders, too. We stood there squeezing each other, smiling like idiots.

I can't get that woman out of my head. Seizing in the aisle. And the perm guy, I just couldn't fucking take it anymore, but what if Ricardo had taken too long pulling me off him and that woman had choked on her own spit?

Ricardo saved that woman's life. Jonas the Whale couldn't ignore the perm guy, couldn't get past that. Jonas the Whale got into a fight and almost let her die.

Walking up my front yard, I'm planning to go straight inside for the fridge and the beer, but I step on something on the front porch, stop and bend. A yellow padded envelope. I wonder what the fuck this could be, and then I remember and open it right there, shake out the blue and white pack. *Official Movie Photo Cards with 1 Stick Bubble Gum.* Picture of a red planet on the front, hanging in space.

Six cards inside, with scenes from the movie on the front. Captions under the scenes: *Diomedes-1 Lifts Off, Desert Planet, Building the Water Generator, Rebellion!, The Flood, Pod Escape.* There's a pink stick of gum stuck to the back of the last card. I peel it off, hold it up, sniff it. Smells like gum. Put it in my mouth and chew. It breaks apart into hard pieces, but I finally force it into a chewy ball. Tastes like gum.

I dig out my notebook and try writing.

I want to beat the shit out of somebody right now.

What did Connie say? Draw a line. Trigger—Action. So I draw a wobbly line and try to remember why.

Brian Lang's on the TV, smiling into the camera.

We've got Sara Jane on the line from Wichita. Hello, Sara Jane.

Hello, Brian. I'm so glad I got through.

We're glad to have you. What are you interested in tonight?

The figurines.

Davey or Goliath?

Goliath, for sure.

I moved the TV from the living room into the bedroom. Deb has these little ceramic teddy bears that her parents get her each Christmas, and they're all lined up on a shelf in the living room. They each have a costume that represents different parts of her personality: salesgirl bear, track-and-field bear, chef bear. It got impossible to watch *Collectors' Corner* with those stupid bears smiling and staring.

I think Davey and Goliath set such wonderful examples for children, Sara Jane says. I wish they were still on the air.

Brian says, I couldn't agree with you more.

I fan the trading cards out on the bed, arranging them one way, then another, trying to see if I can get them to tell a story. Chewing, sucking the sugar out of the gum.

What did she see, that woman? I see it, I see it, she'd said, right before she had the seizure. What did she see?

I take the phone into the bedroom so I can see the TV. I almost hang up when the operator asks for my name, almost chicken out, but when she asks again I tell her and she says to please hold, she's going to put me on the air.

We have Jonas on the line from Los Angeles. Hello, Jonas.

Hey.

What can we do for you tonight?

Do you remember me?

I do now, Brian says. I recognize your voice.

I got those cards in the mail today.

And what did you think?

You mean, do I get it?

Do you?

I look at the cards, the TV. I don't know, I say.

You didn't eat the gum did you?

I did.

You did? Brian's smiling again now. How was it?

It wasn't too bad, Brian.

Brian laughs. You're a brave man, Jonas.

I don't feel so brave.

Pardon me?

I don't say anything. Brian stares into the camera, eyebrows raised.

Jonas?

A woman almost died at work tonight, I say.

Oh, Brian says. I'm sorry to hear that. Is she all right?

I think so. One of the other guys poured orange juice down her throat.

Where do you work, Jonas?

At a supermarket. I'm a checkout clerk at a supermarket.

I'm sorry to hear that. About the woman. I really am.

Yeah, I say. I guess I was pretty upset.

I can see where you would be. Brian looks into the camera, nodding, almost like he's waiting for me to calm down.

Stay with us, Jonas, he says. We're going to have a good show tonight.

The big news at class is that Luis was in a high-speed chase this morning and got arrested. The neighbors heard his girlfriend screaming and called the cops. He was hitting her with a shoe and the cops came and he ran out the back door and got in his truck and drove off through the neighbor's lawn. He got on the freeway and went up through downtown and then back through Hollywood, driving on the shoulder around the stopped traffic until they got him with one of those wheel-spike strips and he blew out his tires and had to hoof it. He jumped over the side wall of the freeway and rolled down the hill and started hauling ass but he was missing a shoe and they got him.

The Traffic Guy was covering the whole thing from his helicopter and he tells us the story. Connie watches the Traffic Guy and listens and when he's done she asks, What was that like?

What was what like? the Traffic Guy says.

Reporting about someone you know who has the same problems you do.

While it was happening.

Connie nods.

It felt like I was betraying him, the Traffic Guy says. Honestly, at first, I wanted him to get away. I felt like, somehow, if he got away then it wouldn't be so bad. That what he did wouldn't seem so bad. But everybody back in the studio, the anchors and producers were all so disgusted by him, by what he had done, and they were rooting for the cops so I started rooting for the cops, too. I felt like shit for wanting him to get away. Like that made me just as bad as he was. I got so upset they had to mute me. I hope they get that fucker, I said. It almost got on the air.

Everyone's agitated in the cafeteria. The story has charged the room. Luis should have been caught, but he shouldn't have been caught. I should have been caught, but I shouldn't have been caught. No one wants to be on TV, running from the cops. No one wants to be the thing people watch in the morning as they get ready for work.

Connie says, What are you all doing to make sure this doesn't happen to you? Her voice is shaking and that adds to the agitation.

This is important, she says. We're going around the room and you tell me what you're doing.

The middle manager guy says, I'm writing in my notebook.

The Traffic Guy says, I'm writing in my notebook.

Fabio says, I'm writing in my notebook.

Spooked. Everybody's spooked. Everybody waves their notebooks in the air, warding it off, keeping it away.

Grandma knew what to do, when I got in the red. Grandma knew what to do and then the fall in the shower and then the home.

Deb knew what to do. Deb knew what to do and then of course she didn't.

I'm writing in my notebook, we say, waving them in the air. I'm writing in my notebook, I'm writing in my notebook.

I'm writing in my notebook. I wanted to watch *Collectors' Corner*, but the cable is out. Sometimes it gets so hot in the summer that the TV just takes a shit. That and I keep finding Deb's long black hairs on the pillowcases, so I went out onto the porch and started writing in my notebook. Just stupid shit about the day, watching the late night cars speed across the freeway overpass, trying to remember what I'd been doing this morning when Luis had passed over it getting chased by the cops.

We have Jonas on the line from Los Angeles. Hello, Jonas.

Hey, Brian.

Having a good night, I hope.

I've had better.

I know the feeling.

My TV's out.

How are you watching the show?

I'm not. I'm out on my porch.

Getting some air.

I guess so.

Well, we've got bears tonight, Jonas.

Bears.

They're authentic *Star Trek* bears. Hand-molded ceramic. They're costumed like Captain Kirk, Spock, the whole crew.

I want to hang up. Through the screen door, I can see Deb's bears on their shelf in the living room.

Instead, I say, I have some of those bears already.

Brian says, You have the *Star Trek* bears?

No, they're different bears.

Well these bears are brand new, Jonas. Just released. The whole *Star Trek* crew.

How do they look?

Oh, they look great, Jonas. They have a lot of personality.

After a second, I say, Okay, I'll order one.

Which one?

You pick, Brian. Whichever one you think.

I'll do that, Jonas. I'll put you on with an operator. Have a good night.

Brian.

Yes?

When I'm waiting for an operator, they play your show instead of music.

Yes, they do.

Could someone keep me on hold for the rest of the show, seeing as my TV's on the fritz?

I don't see why not, Jonas. I think that can be arranged.

Okay. Thanks.

Thank you, Jonas. Stay with us.

But sometimes, the Traffic Guy says, you have to do something. Sometimes a response is called for.

But not a violent response, Connie says. There's always another way.

Not always.

Yes, always. A violent response just leads to another violent response.

The Traffic Guy really has a bug up his ass tonight. What is this? he says. *The Cycle of Violence?*

That's one name for it.

I've heard it a million times. *Breaking the Cycle of Violence.*

A police siren, out of nowhere, the sound smearing as it passes the cafeteria. Everybody flinches except Connie.

Sometimes, Connie says, you hear things a million times because they're true.

Sometimes, the Traffic Guy says, you hear things a million times because they're bullshit.

Hey man calm down, the middle manager says.

Don't tell me to calm down. He looks back at Connie. What if you're in a fight, he says. Somebody attacks you and you do nothing. You stand and get pummeled. You stand and get killed.

You want to fight back.

Fuck yes, the Traffic Guy says. You have to defend yourself.

None of you are here for defending yourselves, Connie says.

Another siren through the open windows, front of the room to the back.

Fuck you, Connie.

I will ask you to leave.

For speaking my mind.

For speaking your mind in an abusive manner I will ask you to leave.

I apologize.

Don't patronize me.

I fucking apologize, Miss Connie. Miss Perfect Connie. I am so sorry.

Leave.

I'm leaving.

Leave.

The night after Deb left, her dad showed up at the house. It was about three in the morning and I heard someone shouting from the front lawn so I went out onto the porch and it was Deb's dad. He was standing on the other side of the fence yelling at the house. Come out here you son of a bitch. Come out here you batterer. He looked pretty ridiculous, this old guy standing there in a golf shirt and shorts with his socks pulled up to his knees, yelling at the house.

Go home, I said. You don't know what you're talking about.

You son of a bitch, he said. I know what I'm talking about. I'm talking about her face. What you did to her face.

I didn't do nothing to her face.

You son of a bitch.

He pulled open the gate and ran up the walkway, onto the porch, took a swing. He missed by a mile and I pushed him back, sprawling onto the lawn in his golf shirt and shorts and socks. Three o'clock in the morning. Some old man lying in the dirt, breath knocked out of him, looking like he was going to cry.

That's my little girl you son of a bitch and if you ever go near her again I'll kill you.

He got up and limped back to his car. I got a beer out of the fridge and sat on the porch and drank. I was really in the red then. If I'd had my notebook then, I would have written down that I wanted to kill Deb's dad. And I would have drawn a line and written that the reason I wanted to kill him was because I would have done the same thing if I were him and some fucking monster had done that to my little girl's perfect face.

When I get home from work, the first thing I notice is that no one's stolen the TV from the front porch yet. The second thing I notice is a padded envelope by the door. I don't even wait to go inside. I turn on the porch light and open the envelope.

There it is, the "Bones" McCoy bear. Hand-molded ceramic. Holding a small medicine vial in one paw, squinting at the liquid inside.

The phone rings. I unlock the door and go in.

Someone whispering on the phone, Turn on your TV. Turn on your TV to Channel Four.

Who is this?

This is Bob Shed. Turn on your TV to Channel Four. I'm calling everyone.

Who's Bob Shed?

From the class, he says. Bob Shed from the class. I sit behind where Luis used to sit.

The middle manager guy.

What's on Channel Four? I say.

Just turn it on and you'll see.

I pull the phone cord out onto the porch and turn on the TV. Brian Lang is holding up an autographed poster from the TV show *Quantum Leap*. I turn to Channel Four.

There's a helicopter shot of a pretty nice-looking house, Beverly Hills or Bel Air or somewhere. A spotlight from another helicopter, a police helicopter, moves back and forth across the front lawn and roof of the house. Squad cars block the street, a couple of cops stand in the driveway pointing their guns. The Traffic Guy's kneeling in front of the house, hands in the air. The graphic on the bottom of the screen says *Breaking News*.

Do you see it? Bob Shed says.

I see it, I say. I see it.

There was a standoff, he says. He was in there with his wife and daughter and a handgun. The daughter's like six years old. That's his own traffic copter filming that shot.

I feel like I'm going to be sick. I don't say this to Bob Shed, but I feel it.

I can't believe it, Bob Shed says. That's two of us in two weeks. Who's next, do you think? Who's going to be next?

I've got to go, I say.

Me too, Bob Shed says. I've got to call the rest of the class.

On the TV, the cops have the Traffic Guy lying face-down on his porch, hands behind his head. One cop's got his knee in the Traffic Guy's back while another cop cuffs him. The wife and daughter come out of the house and a cop pulls a blanket over their shoulders and leads them to a squad car. Big group of neighbors on the sidewalk across the street. They clap for the wife and daughter as they pass by.

* * *

I have this dream where Luis and the Traffic Guy and Brian Lang and I are on a talk show, and Connie is the host. Luis is wearing handcuffs and an orange prison jumpsuit. The Traffic Guy is wearing the same thing. We're all sitting in a row on a stage in front of an audience and Connie asks us what it's like to be TV stars. Luis and the Traffic Guy and Brian Lang all say that they like it all right, and then Connie asks me what it's like to be a TV star. I say I've never been on TV and Brian says, But your voice has, Jonas, and Luis smiles and says, You'll be on soon enough, man. You'll be on soon enough.

The assignment this week, Connie says, is the toughest one. And if you don't think you can do it safely, you are not to attempt it. I can't emphasize this enough. Is that understood?

Everybody nods.

This week, Connie says, I want you to look through your notebooks and find a situation that set you off back at the beginning of the class. Something that you became angry about. And I want you to put yourself in that situation again.

Some raised eyebrows here in the cafeteria.

You all need to be able to deal with situations that have the potential to set you off, she says. You're going to encounter them all the time once the class is over, and you and I both need to be confident that you can deal with those situations in a safe and responsible manner.

A guy in the back says, Even after Luis.

Even after Luis.

Even after the Traffic Guy.

You are not Luis, Connie says. You are not the Traffic Guy.

This is like our final exam, the middle manager says. Bob Shed.

Yes, Connie says. This is like your final exam.

This is Deb's TV, I say. I brought Deb her TV back.

I'm calling the police you son of a bitch. Get away from my house.

Deb's dad shouts at me through his screen door. I can see Deb and her mom's faces in an upstairs window, watching.

I'm on the phone right now you son of a bitch, he yells. I dialed nine-one-one.

I just want to give her back her TV.

Deb's not coming out you son of a bitch. Deb wants nothing to do with you.

Then can you come out and get the TV.

Dogs barking. Lights snapping on in windows along the street.

Deb's mom calls from the upstairs window, Carl don't, but Deb's dad puts down the phone and comes charging through the screen door. He's carrying a golf club. A nine iron, looks like. Maybe a seven.

You son of a bitch, you won't lay a hand on my little girl again do you hear me?

He's running down the lawn, cocking the club over his shoulder. I'm gripping the TV so hard the corners are cutting into my hands. Ten steps away. I can feel the roll of quarters in my pocket. Leave them, leave them. Five steps away. Keep gripping the TV. You are not Luis, you are not the Traffic Guy. Maybe, Connie, maybe. One step away, Deb's dad plants his feet.

Never again you son of a bitch, he says. Do you hear me?

I hear you, I say, I hear you, and I clench my teeth and keep gripping the TV so that I don't do anything, I don't cover up or hit back or even make a sound when Deb's dad starts swinging.

About halfway home I find a pay phone with its receiver still attached.

We have Jonas on the line from Los Angeles. Hello, Jonas.

Hello, Brian.

How's your night?

I've had better.

I hear you, my friend. Something on the show caught your eye?

My eye. My left eye is too swollen shut to see.

I'm not watching the show, I say.

Your TV's out again.

I gave it back. It wasn't my TV.

Brian laughs. How do you like the bear? The *Star Trek* bear.

It's great, Brian. It's just like you said it would be.

Our connection is bad, Brian says. Where are you, Jonas?

I'm at a pay phone.

Are you all right?

What do you have on the show?

Are you all right, Jonas?

What do you have on the show.

Resin models. A Godzilla model and a Mothra model.

A lot of people are calling in.

They are.

I'll take one of those models.

Which one?

You pick.

They take a while to paint, you know.

That's okay.

I wipe something out of my eyes. Blood from my head, a throbbing cut somewhere under my hair.

Brian says, Maybe you should go home, Jonas.

I will, I say. In a while. But I'd like to listen. I'd like to go on hold and listen to the show.

From a pay phone.

I got a whole roll of quarters.

Jonas?

I'd just like to listen to the show for a while, Brian, before I go home.

Okay, Jonas, he says. Stay with us.

All right, I say. I'll try.

Flicker

Occasionally, he was recognized. In line at the supermarket, sitting alone in a diner, piloting the airport shuttle. Strangers' eyes up in the rearview mirror from one of the seats behind, trying to place his face.

They remembered the laundry detergent commercials, the antismoking PSAs. They remembered *L.A. Heat*, the police procedural on which George guest-starred for a season in the early '80s. Sometimes they misremembered him as another actor who was the same age then that George was now, a graying, creased character player with a face that held a kind of battered dignity. When George was feeling up to it, he corrected them. They were folding time back into itself, he would say. He was a young man in the year they were thinking. He hadn't always been this old.

Sometimes they remembered the movie. Young people, especially. These kids had seen it all; so much was available on their computers, their phones. They took a competitive pride in the obscurity of their interests. George could see victory in their faces when they remembered the title of the film. They started typing immediately, snapping pictures, sending out proof of their find.

Thalassa, they said. Weren't you in that movie?

To George, it wasn't a question, it was an accusation. Thirty years ago, the movie had played in theaters across the country. George was the leading man—his first and only role in a major studio film. It had opened with a brief, energized sprint, but then faltered quickly, disastrously. Stumbling through July, crawling through August. By Labor Day it was showing at odd hours in odd locations. Newspaper ads shrank from full to half to a quarter page, then to a single line tacked on to another movie's announcement, the back end of a bargain double feature.

Over the years it had developed some kind of minor cult status. A curiosity, a joke, a cautionary tale. George had heard that film professors discussed it in budgeting classes, the perils of spending too much on too little.

Checking out a book at the library, drinking a cup of coffee in a cafe, they approached him, warily at first, but gaining a brazen confidence as they grew more certain. He'd answer for the commercials and the TV show and the PSAs, but when they called out the title of the movie he denied it.

I'm not who you think I am, he'd say. You must have me confused with someone else.

He was having a sandwich at the shuttle depot when his agent called with news of a remake. She said that the studio was restarting what it now called the "franchise," planning a new version of the film as a summer blockbuster.

"They want me to be involved?" George said, before she could go any further. He had almost forgotten the little surge of hope that could come from answering the phone. He hadn't been offered a part in years.

"Oh God, no," she said. "That's the last thing they want."

The studio, she told him, was going to make the original movie disappear once and for all. *Burning the baggage*, is how they described it. They were recalling home video versions, scouring the internet for clips and pirated streams. By the time the new film opened, there would be nothing left of the old, just a smoothed-over patch of collective memory, an entire summer repaved.

"Is that even possible?" George said. He imagined all those kids with their websites and newsfeeds, endlessly clicking, relinking, echoing.

There was a crunching on the other end of the line. Lunchtime. Salad croutons, it sounded like.

"With enough money and lawyers," his agent said, "you can make anything go away."

He had received the news that he had been cast in the original film while standing in a phone booth on Franklin Avenue. An afternoon in late spring, thirty years before. George's agent had been trying to reach him all day. The phone upstairs in George's apartment was dead; the line chewed by squirrels walking the wire.

Three weeks later he was on set, baking in the desert in the impossible costumes, the helmets, the boots and gloves. Trying to get into his character amidst all the distractions, the gigantic cast and strange vehicles and hundreds upon hundreds of takes. At night he sat in his motel room, stripped naked in the heat, reading the script and trying to inhabit this man, Dean, a scientist, a pioneer courageous enough to leave every certainty behind, to follow his ideas and passions to an unknown world. It was a leap for George; he had never thought of himself as brave, as someone who sacrificed for a dream. But finally, late one night in the delirious heat, exhausted, nearly defeated, he realized that this is exactly who he was, who he had willed himself to be. This is what he was doing with his own life. He had moved to Los Angeles, he had auditioned and waited tables and endured rejection and indifference, he had already taken that leap, and finally he was here, Dean was here, to make something of that dream.

The shoot ended in mid-autumn, the first week of colder nights. George returned to his apartment early one evening and set down his suitcases and turned on every light in the place, a boy afraid of the dark. How small and bare it seemed now, the stale air, the windows that shook in their casings when a bus passed on the street below. He felt as if he had become a different man in the vastness of the desert. These were now a stranger's rooms.

He turned and walked back out, driving aimlessly, eventually ending up in Los Feliz at the storefront theater where he had taken acting classes since first arriving in town. He was welcomed like a visiting dignitary. Other students crowded around, asking for details from the set. They wanted to know what it was like to finally achieve what they were all striving for.

George didn't know what to say. He was surprised by how disarmed he felt. The richness of the experience in the desert had started to fade as soon as he'd returned to L.A., like a hallucination, or a mirage. The finished film wouldn't arrive for months; he had no proof yet of what he had done out there, what they had made. So instead, he related little bits of petty gossip—who was difficult to work with, who was sleeping with whom—and when the excitement died down he sat alone in the last row, trying to fade back to anonymity. He watched the exercises and scene work, feeling so out of place, so alien, and then a young man, a new student, crossed to the center of the stage and gave his name.

George could still recall James in those first moments: tall and slim, with dark eyes and darker hair combed back from his high forehead. He looked like a Wall Street wonder boy, or what George imagined a Wall Street wonder boy might look like. A junior executive from some 1950s car ad, gleaming, precise, confident. It was as if he had stepped out of George's childhood memory, one of his father's polished colleagues stopping by the house after work for a drink.

George watched, enraptured, for the rest of the night. He was captivated by James's composure in a scene or a Meisner exercise, standing face-to-face with another student, each repeating what the other said until boredom or emotion drove one of them to change the inflection or phrase. James was fearless. Nothing fazed him: displays of affection, revulsion, anger. He knew who he was, and was unafraid to let others see.

George continued to attend class, partly because he was feeling uncertain again about his abilities, but mostly to see James. As the weeks went on, they began sitting together in the theater, then they were going for coffee after, gossiping about the other students or their instructor, a woman more than twice their age who was rumored to have once dated Cary Grant. But despite their growing connection, neither of them made a move. It seemed to George as if James was waiting for him to act first, as if James expected to be pursued, but George held back. The confidence he had found in the desert was wearing off. He was reverting, turning back to who he'd been before.

One night they ran into each other at a club in Silver Lake. Both were with other groups of friends, and surprised to encounter one another. It was the first time George had seen James blush. By the end of the evening, they were both drunk, sitting together at the bar. James leaned in and told George that he had a confession to make.

"I've been waiting for you to ask the right questions." He yelled to be heard above the Bee Gees on the bar's overdriven sound system. "But I might die of old age first, so I'll just come clean." He put his arm around George's shoulder and smiled. "I'm not an actor," he said. "I'm a grad student at UCLA. Psychology. I'm taking the acting class for a project I'm working on." George could feel James smile as his lips brushed George's ear. "It's an undercover mission."

George turned to look at James, surprised. James was such a good actor.

"Now you're going to out me," James yelled. He leaned in close again. "What do I have to do to keep you quiet?"

At night now, when he didn't have the late shuttle shift, George sat at the desk in his bedroom and used his aging computer to search online. His agent had been right: The movie was disappearing. Each time he looked, fewer search results surfaced. Clips and scenes and trailers had vanished. Scanned pages of the script, production designs, photographs of the actors in their costumes—one night he was able to access them, the next they were gone. He thought of saving what he could still find onto his hard drive, but it seemed a futile gesture. Who would he be saving it for? Who would care to see?

One night, a week past the call from his agent, the search engine returned nothing but other meanings of the movie's title, sites for Greek mythology and menus from seaside restaurants. George continued clicking, almost in a panic, finally finding a reference several pages deep—an old, scathing newspaper review from that summer, a discovery that once would have saddened or enraged him, but which now brought a small, desperate feeling of relief. George left the review up on his screen, watching it from his bed like a nightlight.

The next morning, George woke to find his screen darkened with its own sleep. When he clicked it awake and refreshed the browser, the review was gone.

* * *

James was having problems with his roommates and had moved out of his place in Westwood. He spent a week or so on various friends' couches before George asked him to move into the apartment on Franklin.

They did some redecorating, buying a few prints for the walls, movie one-sheets from *Rebel Without a Cause* and *Blow-Up*. James picked out throw rugs, adjusted the angles of the furniture, covered the television with a red chenille throw and set a potted cactus on top. James didn't care for TV; it was movies that he loved. Movies were art to James, or at least held the possibility of art. They left an impression in the world, created a communal experience, people sitting together in a dark room, sharing focus.

Their first argument occurred when George told James that he couldn't bring him along to the movie's premiere. "Can't or won't?" James had asked. "Both," George said. He was anxious not only about finally seeing the film, but about the attention it might bring, the cameras and questions. His career was just getting started, and it would be too much to have to explain who James was—a friend, not a date.

"Is that what we are?" James said. "Friends?"

"It's not the same for you."

"What does that mean?" James raised his voice. "That because I'm not in a movie, I've got nothing at risk?"

"That's not what I said."

"I'm asking you to be brave. To be honest."

"It's not that easy," George said.

"I didn't say it was easy." James turned back to the magazine he was reading, briskly flipped a page. "You're afraid," he said, lifting his eyes back up to George, challenging. George looked away and said, "I guess you just know me so well."

At the premiere, George walked the red carpet, smiling away questions about his bachelor status, rumors he was dating the film's lead actress. When the curtain opened and the studio's logo appeared onscreen, he quietly left the auditorium, too nervous to watch. Out in the lobby, he spent the evening talking to the concessions staff, waiting for the auditorium doors to open at the end of the show. He tried to imagine the crowd pouring out, ebullient, buzzing, high from the experience.

Instead, when the movie was over, the audience filed out quietly, their heads down, avoiding eye contact. George accepted compliments from studio executives and other cast members, but their praise felt forced and insincere. In a corner of the lobby, two producers began a heated discussion that quickly turned into a shouting match. They had to be pulled apart by their assistants. The room emptied. It seemed no one could leave too quickly, could create enough distance between themselves and what they had seen on the screen.

When he returned to his apartment that night, the rooms were dark. James was already asleep, or pretending to be. George turned on a light in the living room and opened the script, his constant companion during the months in the desert. A block of white paper shot through with magenta pages, lime, goldenrod,

the rainbow colors of revision, delivered every morning on set
from one of the director's assistants.

George didn't know what the audience had seen in the theater, but he knew what they should have seen. What he had seen,
finally, after wrestling with it for so long, the days under the
unrelenting sun, the sleepless nights in the motel room. He sat
with the script and began reading from the beginning, imagining
the theater dimming at the title page, the audience's conversation
receding to murmurs, then the curtain opening, the projector's
light shining in the dark.

"You look familiar."

The man was George's age, late fifties, Latino, dressed for
business in a sleek gray suit, his black Oxfords gleaming with an
airport shine. He looked up into the shuttle's rearview from his
seat behind George. Their eyes met and George looked away.

"I get that a lot."

The man said, "An actor?"

George shook his head.

The man squinted back up into the mirror, refusing to let it go.

"Somebody famous?" he said. "From a long time back?"

Something caught George's eye then, a word on a theater
marquee on the opposite side of Santa Monica Boulevard. It
pulled his attention from the road, the changing traffic light. He
recovered at the last moment, kicking for the brake pedal, missing, then kicking again and connecting, locking the tires and sliding the last few feet to the lip of the intersection.

"Jesus Christ!" The businessman struggled to connect his seatbelt across his lap.

When the light changed again, George pulled a quick U-turn and drove back on the other side of the street. He parked at the curb and stared at the entrance to the small theater. He'd been right: The phrase he'd seen spelled out in flimsy plastic letters across the center of the marquee was *Diomedes-1*. In the original *Thalassa*, that was the name of his—Dean's—spaceship.

"What the hell are you doing?" the businessman said.

Instead of a movie poster, a large sheet of white paper hung beside the box office window. *Diomedes-1* had been spray-painted through a stencil across the top, guerrilla-art style, and at the bottom was a small drawing of a spaceship, hurtling through the vast white void. Another strip of paper was fixed to the bottom of the makeshift poster, a single string of handwritten dates and times.

The decoy title was code, George realized. The original movie was here, somehow, playing twice a night, this week only.

"Hey!"

The voice jolted George back. He looked up into the rearview mirror. The businessman was strapped tightly to his seat, his expression teetering between panic and anger.

"Are you taking me home," the businessman said, "or not?"

That summer, just before the original movie's release, George rented a house on Cape Cod. It was George and James and their friends Eric and Ted, another couple from acting class who had welcomed George warmly when he was a new student. George paid for the house and the plane tickets, an extravagant gesture, the biggest expenditure of his life to that point. He described it as a celebratory vacation, but what he really wanted was to be away from Los Angeles when the movie opened. He had learned from the audience at the premiere—he was trying to create distance.

The house was just as the owner had described it over the phone, a big weather-beaten box looking out over a long green strip of marsh. The owner was a man in his fifties who seemed the human equivalent of the house: salty and rough-hewn, his face creased from sun and wind. He met them in the gravel driveway and led them on a tour, mostly, it seemed to George, to make the ground rules clear. No loud parties. No drugs. And stay out of the marsh, he said, standing before the French doors at the back of the house, pointing out past the high green reeds to a small cove beyond. A pair of wooden chairs sat arm-to-arm out at the water's edge. All of that, the owner said, belongs to a very private and protective neighbor.

George and James had been on delicate footing since the premiere. The connection between them had been bruised; a dark spot, sore to the touch. James was drawn to conflict, ready for a fight until he was injured, and then he retreated, shutting down almost completely. When James was in that state, George could feel nothing from him. It was as if, in James's eyes, he no longer existed. George would have to draw James back then, slowly, carefully, always with the sense that if he pushed too hard or fast, James would take that final step away.

Slowly, they eased into the pelagic rhythms and routines of vacation. The previous summer's renters had left behind tubes of paint and a pile of small, blank canvases, so in the mornings, while George stretched out on the love seat in the living room and worked through the shelves of maritime-themed novels, James created a new character for himself, a pretentiously successful landscape artist, attempting to paint the scene beyond the open doors. After lunch they floated in the tidal pools at Skaket Beach, or rented bikes and rode the trail up to the bluffs, walking through the tall grass, looking out at the sea. Sometimes Eric and Ted joined them; sometimes they went their own way. In the afternoons they all reconvened on the back deck for drinks, everyone coming up with increasingly outlandish stories about the unseen neighbors and their forbidden chairs.

Neither George nor James mentioned their argument over the premiere, but time and distance from the scene of the fight seemed to soften James's anger. He began a portrait of George, though his figure paintings were worse than his landscapes. They laughed about the finished canvas, George as an indistinct blob on the couch holding a book with a majestically masted clipper on its cover. At least I got the boat right, James said.

They went to bed early; they slept late. They spent hours in the fluffy, oversoft four-poster. Everything in their bedroom was white, the walls and ceiling, the bedclothes, the chairs and dressers. In the mornings, the room blazed with light.

Lying in bed, they played a game called Future Tense; James's invention. What they saw for themselves in five years,

ten, fifty. Inconceivable, the lengths of the lives then before
them.

"You'll star in a sequel to the movie," James said. "Then
another, and another. You'll produce, then direct. You'll stand
at the podium at the Academy Awards, and blow me a kiss on
national TV."

"All your fantasies are of me," George said. They lay shoulder-
to-shoulder, thumbs hooked, looking up at the ceiling fan's lan-
guid spin.

"Yes," James said. "They are."

Someone had tracked a child's growth on the doorframe.
Pencil marks climbed the white molding, short horizontal lines
like railroad ties. Knee height to college, it looked like, a fifteen-
year span. The highest mark was fairly recent, and written in
another hand. The young man finally recording his own height.

"This is our house," James said one morning, during a game
of Future Tense. He was sitting on the edge of the bed, looking
at the doorframe. George lay spread out behind him, a forearm
shading his eyes from the sun. They'd forgotten to pull the curtains the night before.

"This is our house," James said, "and that's our son. We've
lived here for twenty years. We drove him to college last weekend. You cried all the way home."

George punched him gently in the ribs. James gave an over-
dramatic wince.

"Is that so impossible?" James asked.

"Yes," George said. Then, "No."

He opened his fist, laying his hand on James's side, palm against skin.

James put his finger to his lips.

"Shhhh," he whispered. "Listen. It's so quiet in the house now."

Every evening after his shuttle shift, George sat in his car across the street from the theater on Santa Monica Boulevard. A handful of people went in for each show, young men mostly, some wearing T-shirts commemorating other, better-known science fiction films from the era.

George had never seen the movie. He'd thought that in time he might come through the other side of the numbness that suffocated him after Cape Cod, and then he would be ready to see it. But he never came through, not completely, and when he could finally see anything on the other side the movie was gone. It had surfaced a few times over the years, and when it appeared he attacked it in whatever form he found it, surprising himself with his ferocity.

Once on his way to a supermarket checkout, he passed a bin of bargain VHS tapes, a jumble of low-budget movies in cheap cardboard sleeves. He had stopped, almost instinctively knowing what he would find inside. He dug up ten copies of the movie. The cover on the sleeve was not the original poster, but some new, poorly executed artwork that emphasized the boy who had played George's son and had gone on to a moderately successful TV career. The sticker price on each copy was less than the box of cereal George carried in his other hand. He bought all ten tapes, then carried them to the alley behind the supermarket, where he stomped each plastic case apart, pulling free the long ribbons of tape.

Years later, he had seen the listing for the movie on a local station's late-night schedule. From a pay phone, he had called the channel and asked to speak to the programming director. When the man answered, George told him that if the movie showed a bomb would detonate in their building. He hung up the phone and stood shaking in the booth. That night he sat up waiting, the TV the only light in his bedroom. When the hour came another movie appeared onscreen, Martians in flying saucers attacking a small Midwestern town. George sat on the edge of his bed, relieved and ashamed and afraid of himself. Such a strange feeling, fearful of what could happen in a room when he was the only one there.

Now, in his car on Santa Monica Boulevard, he tried to imagine the scene in the near-empty theater. He had seen movies there before, remembered the musty auditorium, the high screen, the old purple curtain worn thin like a pair of jeans at the knees. He tried to imagine his other, projected self, thirty years younger, with a smoother face, darker hair, another name. The man he had become in the desert, briefly. He wondered if the courage of that other man was still apparent, if it could be transferred, absorbed in the light of the movie's projected frame.

On their last night in Cape Cod, after dinner in town, they all sat out on the back deck and Eric made margaritas, heavy on the tequila. Ted had picked up a newspaper in town and they all crowded around to gawk at the ad for a drive-in up in Wellfleet, George's face right there in black and white.

"We should go," James said, more than a little drunk. "We'd be walking in with a real movie star."

Eric and Ted agreed. George tried to argue that they were in no condition to drive, but James called for a vote, a show of hands, and then he and Eric and Ted rushed inside to get cleaned up.

Alone on the back deck, George was surprised by how desperate he felt, how afraid. Since they had arrived on the Cape he had tried not to think of the premiere, the shame he'd sensed from the audience as they left the theater. James would see the movie eventually, George couldn't stop that, but he could postpone it, keep it away from them here, at least. This could remain a safe place, another world of their own where they could imagine a life together, painting, dreaming, following a son's progress up a doorframe.

The others were in the bathroom, brushing teeth and combing hair.

"I have a better idea," George said.

They stopped and turned, curious. George lowered his voice to a conspiratorial stage whisper.

"We should go out." He pointed a thumb over his shoulder. "The cove," he said. "The chairs."

Eric smiled, his sunburned cheeks wrinkling white. Ted nodded along. James needed some convincing, he was set on the movie, so George joined him at the mirror, draping his arm over James's shoulders.

"We'll see the movie," George said, looking at their reflection. Two bodies, so close. His lips brushed James's ear. "As soon as we get home. I promise."

They pulled on their swimsuits, sprayed themselves slick with bug repellant, grabbed a flashlight and the tequila. The marsh water was cool and hip-deep. They kept the flashlight off as they waded, whispering and laughing, jumping at noises in the trees flanking their approach. George led the way, holding the tequila bottle high. He stopped when they reached the opening to the cove. The dark water spread before them, rippling slowly, radar waves that grew to some unseen outer limit. The sky was clear and star-flecked; a bright half-moon sat high above. They stood looking up, breathing deeply. George took a sip from the bottle and passed it to James.

The chairs sat above the reeds on a large, flat-topped rock. George climbed up to the first chair. He sat looking out into the cove, the open water beyond. James sat beside him and took his hand.

Eric paddled out in front of the chairs. "It's deep out here," he whispered. "It drops off quickly."

"Can we jump?" James said.

Eric held his breath, flipped under the water. A moment later he reemerged. "It goes way down. I couldn't find the bottom. We could probably dive."

Ted was first, climbing the rock. He handed James the flashlight as he stepped up onto the arms of the chairs, one foot on each. Lifting his hands to the sky, he gave a soundless primal scream, then plugged his nose and launched up and out, tucking his knees to his chin, grabbing his ankles. The splash cracked the silence and they all stiffened, looking back through the trees toward the neighbor's house. Ted surfaced, gasping and laughing, and Eric shushed him. After a moment, when no lights came on through the trees, George stood up on the chairs, handed James the tequila bottle, and jumped in.

The water was a shock, colder and deeper than he'd expected. George paddled down, reaching for the bottom, finally brushing silt with his fingertips before running out of air and pushing back up. He reemerged into another world, soft and moonlit. He could see Eric's and Ted's heads bobbing a little ways out in the water. They were all looking at James.

James set down the empty bottle and climbed up to jump. George heard a small wet slap when each of James's feet touched the arms of the chairs, the little puddles they had all made there. James lifted his own arms, gave a silent, head-shaking shout, its length and ferocity surprising, the release of what looked to George like rage or frustration. He wanted to ask James what this was, if it matched some of what George had felt earlier in the house, his desire to protect something they couldn't really have, but then James squatted on the chair arms, ready to spring out, and one foot left the wood but the other slid in the puddle and he fell back, his head hitting the seat and then the edge of the rock, a sharp snap and a dull thud, and then he was gone, underwater, leaving the surface rippling, dark rings in the moonlight.

George dove under immediately, grasping, but there was nothing, just water. When he came up for air, Eric was coming up, too.

"I couldn't get him," Eric said. "He's way down there."

They went under again. George opened his eyes, but there was only inky black, swirling shadows, vague shapes. He swam down until he touched silt again, pushing himself along the floor, reaching, coming away with nothing but handfuls of mud. Then, finally, a limb, an ankle. George didn't know if it was Eric or James but he pulled hard, swimming up toward the surface.

It seemed like hours, a timeless expanse, climbing, reawakening from a dream.

Then, air and moonlight. George gasped, filling his lungs, and then Eric was there, and Ted. They dragged James back to the rock, lifting him up. They laid him flat and George took James's face gently to clear his mouth, to start resuscitation, but his hands came away glassy with blood.

Eric was already running back, splashing through the marsh toward the lights of their house. Ted turned on the flashlight and followed, shining its beam for a path. George stayed with James, quiet for a moment, until that silence grew too loud and he had to break through it, screaming for help.

The neighbors reached the scene first. A husband and wife, middle-aged but tanned and fit, she in a bathrobe, he in pajamas. The wife ran back to the house to call an ambulance. The man stayed, standing hip-deep in the marsh beside the rock, a fist up at his mouth, his face hard, unreadable. George knelt beside James, holding his head, pressing on the wound with his fingers, talking to him, pleading in the cool night air.

The doctors said that James had died on impact. It was the first hit that killed him, his head striking the chair. George could tell that this information was intended to comfort, to assure him that James hadn't suffered, hadn't spent those eternal minutes suffocating underwater, hoping for rescue.

James's parents arrived to bring his body back to St. Louis. They flew in overnight, and the next morning came to the rented house to collect James's things. George had never met them. James didn't like to talk about his strained relationship with his parents, the difficult phone calls and infrequent visits. They were older than George had pictured, and looked more like grandparents: gray, a little shrunken. James was their only child and they'd had him later in life.

James's mother moved through the bedroom gathering books and clothes. When she saw James's canvases she stopped, looking at the blurry landscapes, his unidentifiable portrait of George. Finally she said, "Are these his?" and when George nodded she set them on the pile of books and clothes.

She never looked at the bed. She never looked at George, who stood just outside the doorway. He wanted to ask what she imagined they did there, how she imagined that they lived. Would she believe they were asleep by ten most nights, exhausted from sun and salt water? That they spent the mornings on the back deck with their breakfast and their books?

That her son had died like a child, jumping from something he never should have climbed?

James's father stayed out in his rental car, the engine running, radio news so loud the muffled voices of the announcers pushed through the rolled-up windows. George watched from the house. The man's hands never left the steering wheel.

After they were gone, George went back to the bedroom. He tried to find any trace of James, but all that was left was his toothbrush in a glass by the bathroom sink, its bristles still caked with flecks of dried paste. George lifted the toothbrush out, then sat on the edge of the bed, holding it tightly. When he finally let go, his palm was pocked sore where the bristles had bitten his skin.

After each shuttle shift he searched online, but found only new, younger faces; images of more impressive technology, locations, sets. He typed in all of the names he could remember, cast and crew, but there were no links to that lost world. He typed in his own name, but stopped before sending the request, afraid now of what he wouldn't find.

The night was warm; the air retained an echo of the day's sun-streaked heat. George sat in his car across from the theater on Santa Monica. He had been drinking at a hotel bar down by the airport, but the weightlessness gained from the gin had worn off on the drive north. His body was heavy now, every joint and limb.

He kept the window down, the radio low. A scientist on the news was talking about the NASA rover on Mars. A month or so earlier, the machine had discovered icy white patches in the Martian soil, but now those patches had disappeared. The scientist believed they had phased from ice to vapor without ever becoming water. A rare occurrence, he said. *Sublimation* was the word he used to describe it.

It was nearly time for the later showing. George hadn't seen anyone go into the theater. This was the final night of the movie's run. Tomorrow, another would open; a classic this time, famous faces. The new poster was already up.

His hands ached. Sometimes, he could still feel that toothbrush pressing into the skin of his palm. Such a common thing at the strangest times. Driving the shuttle, or, over the years, mornings with other boyfriends, other men. Standing at the mirror in someone else's bathroom and having to look at his hands to reassure himself nothing was there.

He had thought this would fade with time and it had, but not entirely. It had just grown duller, an ache instead of a burn. It was the one constant in his life. He had carried it through all of his jobs and relationships. There were times he had wanted it gone and times he was afraid it had left him. But it was always there. It had never turned into anything else.

Horns honked as he crossed the street, the sound smearing in the air behind him. Screeching brakes, angry shouts. At the ticket booth, he slid his money through the slot in the cloudy Plexiglas. In the lobby, he walked past the concessions, the smell of old carpet and hot popcorn, and then into the theater, the cool, dim room.

He was alone. He sat and then the room darkened even further and the curtain swung open to free the screen. From above and behind, he heard the projector whirl to life. The first bright light crossed the room, the beam rich with dust. The studio logo, the fanfare. He didn't have to watch. If he let it, the film would pass, one last time, unobserved. He closed his eyes, weak again, shutting it all out. But then he could feel that pressure in his palm, the pain of the bristles refusing to let him slip away. He squeezed back, holding his fist tight, until the pain turned, softening, spreading, and then George could feel warmth from the seat beside him, the pressure in his palm becoming that familiar hand in his.

He opened his eyes and the movie began.

Soldiers

My dad and his friends spent Saturdays drinking. Twenty years before, they'd all gone to high school up in Eagle Rock, and Denny and Rey still lived in their old neighborhood, a few blocks from the bridges crossing the arroyo into Pasadena. Denny and Rey had each been divorced a couple of times and finally ended up just buying a place together. Their house needed what my dad called a shit-ton of work. Every Saturday morning he told my mom he was going over to help them with the house, and Mom would give him that wrinkled, sour-mouthed look, like, *Yeah, right.* Around dinnertime he'd come home, blotchy-faced and weaving, and she'd ask him what they'd worked on and he'd laugh and say about a case apiece. Then he'd get really quiet and just stand in the kitchen, swaying a little in his work boots, staring at her, as if daring her to say something else. Usually, she didn't. She knew better than to push it when he was like that.

My dad worked on crews for movies and TV shows, driving actors and equipment around the set. By that Saturday in May, though, a couple of weeks before I turned twelve, he'd been out of work for months. My mom had to drive up to the farm stand in Santa Clarita and ask for her job back. "I had to practically beg them," she told us. "I had to just about get down on my knees so I could sell fruit by the freeway."

That Saturday morning, my mom didn't know what to do with me. I was supposed to be grounded, but I couldn't go to work with her and I knew she didn't want me hanging out with my dad at Denny and Rey's. She wouldn't let me stay home alone because the last time she'd done that, when my dad was away on a movie shoot, I'd set off an M-80 in the backyard and the garage roof caught fire. The neighbors saw the smoke and called 911. My mom was grocery shopping and when she got home the fire trucks were just leaving. As they pulled away, one of the firefighters leaned out the window of the cab and told her to keep a better eye on her kid.

We stood together in the kitchen, and she looked at me, holding her car keys, already late for the farm stand. We could hear my dad calling from out in the driveway, ready to leave. Mom looked like she was going to scream or cry.

"Frank," she said, "what can I do?"

I didn't know what to say, if I was supposed to answer or not. But then she pushed her lips together and shook her head.

"Just go," she said. She sounded resigned, like she'd had enough of him, of me. Like she was finally giving up.

The day before, my mom and I sat in the principal's office with little Curt Lin and his parents. Curt's parents were both tall and thin, well dressed, his dad in a dark suit and his mom in a jacket and skirt and heels. My mom was wearing the denim shirt and jeans she wore up at the farm stand. She kept her hands folded in her lap, covering the raggedy, bitten ends of her fingernails.

Curt's mom told the principal that Curt didn't want to go to school because his stomach hurt so much in the mornings. They hadn't been able to figure out what was wrong. They'd even taken him to the doctor for tests. When nothing came back he finally told them the truth.

Neither of his parents looked at me or my mom when they spoke, but I could feel how angry they were. It was like heat in the room. Curt's dad told the principal I either needed to leave Curt alone or I should be kicked out of school. The principal said that wasn't how things worked, but she would see to it that I didn't go near him anymore. She told me to apologize. I looked at the scuffed toes of my sneakers and said I was sorry. "Eyes, Frank," the principal said, so I turned to Curt and his parents to say it again, but as I started to speak they all turned away.

Driving home from the principal's office, my mom stared out the windshield, her fists tight around the steering wheel, knuckles round and white like little sand dunes. Neither of us spoke, until finally she said, "What's wrong with you, Frank? Why would you do those things to him? Do you like when those things are done to you?"

"No," I said, but maybe my voice was too low. It didn't seem like she heard me.

"I didn't want you to go this way," she said. She still wouldn't look at me. Nobody would look at me—Curt, his parents, my mom. "I didn't want you to be like him." Like my dad, she meant. She'd said this before, but it wasn't until later that night, home in bed, that I realized what was different this time. Before she had always said, "I *don't* want you to be like him," and this time she'd said *didn't*. Like it was too late now—it was a done deal.

My mom had the car, so my dad and I took the bus up to Eagle Rock. I was wearing the helmet my dad had given me when he got back from his last movie shoot. It was a new version of an old space movie that took place on this desert planet. All these scientists had gone there from Earth to try and see if they could create water so people could live there, but there was this other group of people, these terrorists, who were trying to destroy the water machine, so the scientists had a bunch of military guys guarding things. The helmet was part of a guard costume. It was sort of tannish orange, the color of sand, with a cool-looking insignia, the silhouette of this ancient armored warrior inked onto the front. With the chin straps tightened all the way, it fit pretty well. I wore it just about all the time when I was home. I think my dad liked to see it on me. It seemed to put him in a good mood. When he'd first given it to me, I asked him if it was a gift from the movie's director or something, if everyone had gotten one. He looked at me like I was the biggest idiot in the world and then laughed through his nose and rapped me on the side of the helmet. Nobody else got one, he said. This was the only helmet that left the set.

We got off at a stop on Colorado Boulevard. It had rained a

little the night before, and now a fog hung just overhead, like a gray layer of cotton, wet to the touch. We passed a wine shop and an art gallery, and then a bakery on the corner. I could smell fresh bread and cookies as we walked by the windows, steamed from the warmth inside.

When we reached their house, Denny and Rey were sitting in plastic lawn chairs on the little cement porch, drinking. "Started early," my dad said, swinging the front gate open, and Denny lit a cigarette and said, "Don't you know it."

For a while, before they'd bought their own place, Denny and Rey had come over to our house almost every weekend to watch boxing or cage fighting on TV. My mom didn't like them coming around, but when my dad had a job he could always say that he was the one who paid the bills, so who he chose as guests in his house was his business.

Denny was a big guy, with a round, shaved head. He had giant teeth, yellow because he smoked. Rey was shorter and skinnier, and Mexican, I think, though when I asked my dad once he said that Rey was American like everybody else. Rey didn't talk much. He had a thin, wiry mustache, and dark eyes, almost black. He drank more than my dad and Denny combined, barely swallowing the gulp of beer in his mouth before tipping the can back up to his lips.

My dad was right: Denny and Rey's house needed a shit-ton of work. The stucco was cracked and peeling, the roof sagged, the windows were old and thin and pocked in the corners from what looked like BBs or buckshot. The houses on either side were in about the same condition, but I could see that things got nicer farther up the street. Up there the lawns were green and mowed, the paint was smooth and bright, the cars in the driveways were newer hatchbacks and hybrids. About halfway up the hill I could see three kids, two boys and a girl, playing in the front yard of one of the renovated houses. They looked to be around my age. I couldn't see what they were doing, but they were moving around very deliberately, with small parts of something it seemed like they were building or fixing.

My dad looked up where I was looking and said, "Neighborhood's changing."

Denny nodded from the porch. "Lot of white people moving in now," he said.

I said, "Aren't we white people?" and Denny took a pull on his cigarette and said, "Different kind."

An old red pickup sat in Denny and Rey's front yard. Its bed was a jumble of tools, hardware, extension cords. A blue plastic cooler sat in one corner. "Let's get to work," Denny said, and for a second I thought my dad was going to grab a screwdriver or a caulk gun, but instead he popped open the cooler and pulled out a beer and tossed it across the yard to the porch, the can trailing a ribbon of water as it flew. Denny shot up his hand and caught the can. My dad pulled another from the cooler and tossed it the same way. Rey had to lean way out of his chair, almost falling to the ground to catch it before it bounced.

"Jesus, bro," Denny said to my dad. "Your arm's for shit these days."

Rey laughed at this, popped open the beer, began to chug.

My dad grabbed his own beer and joined them on the porch, taking an empty lawn chair. I stood by the chain-link fence surrounding the yard, not sure what to do. I watched those kids playing up the street. I listened to the men talk about high school, the pranks they'd pulled, the girls they'd dated. Whenever I heard a belch and a can crinkling in a fist, I'd open the cooler and deliver another beer.

"You're getting to be a tough-looking fucker," Denny said, after I'd handed him a can. "Can you still take a punch?"

"Try him," my dad said, and Denny cocked his arm, but I backed off the porch before he could swing.

"Smart, too," Denny said, and they all laughed.

The men were getting drunker and louder. Denny wanted to know what the deal was with my helmet, so my dad started talking about the job he'd finished a few months back. He told the men what he'd told me and my mom, about how making a movie out in the desert was like fighting a war, all the people and machines and dust and heat. Before he could get very far, though, Denny held up a hand and told my dad to shut up. He'd been in Iraq, he said, for a real war, and my dad didn't know what the fuck he was talking about.

"Come back up here," Denny said to me then. "I want to see that helmet."

I unclipped the chin strap, lifted the helmet off my head.

"I didn't say to throw it." Denny's stare was level. He looked me right in the eyes. "I said bring it up here."

I clipped the helmet back on and walked toward the porch.

The men waited, watching me. I stepped up onto the cement and closed my eyes because I didn't want to see it coming, didn't want to flinch, and then a big hand hit the side of my helmet and my head jerked and I stumbled off the porch, using the momentum to back even farther away toward the pickup. I didn't want to get caught in that circle again, like back in our living room those times with some cage match on TV and Denny and Rey and my dad sitting on the edge of the couch, pushing and slapping me back and forth, like I was the one in the cage.

"Come on, you little pussy."

I didn't recognize the voice so I opened my eyes and saw that it was Rey who had spoken. He was leaning forward in his chair, like he'd been brought to life by Denny's punch.

"Get back up here," he said.

I backed away until I was on the other side of the truck, hidden from view.

"Come on, Frankie," Denny called. "Don't take it so hard."

I grabbed the top of the fence and pulled myself over onto the other side and started walking up the hill. I could hear Denny calling out a few more times and then laughter from the porch, but by then I was far enough away that their voices were just buzzy noise, blurring with the rotor chop of a police helicopter passing overhead.

Those kids were still out playing in their front yard. Their coloring was lighter than anyone I'd ever seen. The girl was so pale that a thin blue vein was visible running beneath the skin of her cheek. The boys' hair was butter-blond; the girl's was nearly white. They wore what looked to me like school clothes—clean khaki pants and navy-blue collared shirts. They had dragged a picnic table bench out onto the middle of their front lawn, and the boys were kneeling at its side, working at something on top. The girl stood behind them, wrapping what looked like a long length of gauze bandage into a tight ball.

I thought about Curt Lin, the glimpse of him I had once when I passed the nurse's office, the nurse pressing gauze to his bloody lip.

The older boy at the picnic bench said something over his shoulder and the girl laughed; the younger boy smiled. I tried to imagine what it would be like to be one of those kids on their lawn, playing together. To be so clean and light. To be part of a group like that, a team. As I passed their driveway I slowed, hoping they would call out to me, ask my name. I didn't have any friends, even in my own neighborhood. Other kids only paid attention when something was happening like with Curt Lin. They stood around me then, and cheered me on, but the rest of the time they'd barely even look at me.

The girl had finished with the gauze and was filling a metal canteen from a hose attached to the side of the house. The boys had disassembled a couple of toy machine guns on top of the picnic bench. All the parts had been laid out carefully—the stocks and grips and triggers, the bright red plastic tips that were supposed to show that these guns weren't real. The older boy was lifting each part and rubbing it clean with a washcloth, then handing it to the younger boy, who set the part back down in its place.

They were too busy to notice me, so I faked a cough, and

then they all looked up, in order it seemed, the two boys and then the girl.

The older boy called out, "Cool helmet."

I stopped walking and stood at the edge of their lawn.

The boy said, "What's your name?"

"Frankie," I called back. "Frank."

The girl started down the lawn toward me, still holding the canteen. "I'm Brittany," she said, "and this is Luke and this is Liam. Liam and I are twins, but Luke's a year older."

"Sixth grade," Luke said.

"What grade are you in?" Liam said.

"Sixth," I lied. "Like your brother." I didn't like to be around older kids. Even if they were shorter than me, they made me feel small.

Luke looked down the street to where my dad and Denny and Rey were sitting on the porch. "You live with those guys?"

"Just my dad. We don't live here. Those are his friends."

"We're not supposed to go down there," Brittany said. "To that part of the street."

"Where'd you get the helmet?" Luke said.

"It's from a movie."

"I know it's from a movie. We've seen it a bunch of times. That water machine that looks like a giant octopus."

"My dad worked on the set," I said. And then, "He's an actor. He's one of the stars."

Luke nodded. It seemed like he was impressed. He gave Liam a nudge.

"We're about to go out on a mission," Liam said. "You want to come?"

"What kind of mission?" I said.

Luke finished screwing the muzzles onto the plastic guns, leaving off the red warning tips. He lifted a rifle, resting the barrel on his shoulder.

"Like in your dad's movie," he said. "We're the rebel group that wants to blow up the giant water machine." He looked at my helmet. "And you're one of the machine's guards."

Brittany thought about this for a second. "But maybe he's really helping us," she said. "Like he gave us the plans on how to blow it up."

Luke scowled at her. "Why would he do that?"

Brittany shrugged, ready to let the idea drop, but I looked down to Denny and Rey's house, then back to the kids. "Because," I said, "maybe I'm secretly joining your side."

We started up the hill. Brittany wore a pink Hello Kitty backpack, the canteen swinging from a Velcro strap on the side. The boys carried the guns stiffly, muzzles down, the same way I'd seen soldiers carry weapons on TV. Along the way they waved to the adults they saw working on their yards or houses, and the adults waved back and called the kids by name.

At the end of the street we turned off onto a little dirt trail between two yards, passing a couple of younger kids in a sandbox on one side, a man and a woman working in a garden on the other. Luke turned to me and asked what time I needed to be back. When I shrugged, he said, "I mean before your dad gets worried."

"Before dark," I lied. "My dad gets really worried if I'm not home by then."

"Good," Brittany said. "Same for us."

There was a thick line of cypress at the back edge of the yards. Liam went first, holding the branches up so the rest of us could pass through. On the other side was a clearing, wide and flat and soft with clover. A line of electrical towers stood in the center, their tops lost in the fog.

Brittany sat on a rock and unstrapped her backpack. She drank from the canteen, then passed it to Liam, who passed it to Luke, who took a long guzzle and wiped the metal lip on his shirt and then passed it to me. He looked out over the clearing. "Radio silence from now on," he said. "We'll be completely exposed until we get to the other side."

We crossed the clearing toward the closest tower. Walking through the knee-high clover felt like wading through water, our feet lost below. The boys held their rifles high over their heads as they marched. Passing under the first tower, I could hear the low hum of electricity moving above. Luke whispered, "Don't stop," and tapped the steel support with a knuckle. The metal rang where he'd hit, the vibration carrying up the beam and away into the fog.

There was another line of trees on the other side of the clearing, taller and scragglier than the cypress. As we got closer, I could see the pale bark peeling like dead skin. Luke stopped within the tree line and motioned for the rest of us to hurry over. When we were all gathered he whispered again.

"Right through here," he said, "is the water machine. We'll make two teams." He held up a pair of fingers. "Liam and me will take out the guards on the other side. Brittany and you—" He pointed another finger at me.

"Frank," Brittany said, as if maybe he'd forgotten.

"—Brittany and Frank will set the bomb."

Brittany nodded and the boys ran off through the trees, Luke calling out with different bird whistles and Liam responding with the same. After a moment the fog had taken them completely.

"This way," Brittany said. We walked in the opposite direction, into our own patch of fog, and then Brittany's hand was on my arm, tugging me to the ground. "Hold your breath," she whispered. "Here we go."

We each took a gulp of air. She started to crawl, so I followed alongside. After a few moments I felt the landscape open in front of me, sudden space, and Brittany let out her breath and I let out mine and after another few feet I could see again. We stopped crawling and lay with our heads beneath the fog, looking out over the drop down into the arroyo, the steep dirt walls that led to the wide, dry riverbed below.

"We're here," she said. "Come on."

She turned her body in place on the ground, like a crab rotating, then started sliding down the embankment. I was amazed that she didn't care about her clothes. They didn't look like the kind of clothes her parents would appreciate coming home dirty. If my school clothes ever got dirty, I really got it from my dad. Frankie, you think this shit is free? You think I bust my ass so you can piss all over everything? I could hear it in his voice, then in my own—like it was becoming my own thought. I knew that's when things usually started to get ugly, when his voice became mine and I had to get it out, yelling at someone like Curt Lin, or even Brittany. I tried to get the voice out of my head, rapping myself on my helmet to focus back on the mission.

Brittany was about halfway down the embankment, slowing herself expertly with her hands and feet. I turned myself around the same way and followed, but my fingers kept slipping out of the dirt. It felt like I was going to fall. Brittany was a few lengths below. She reached the bottom and I looked down and she looked up and said, "Don't look down." I turned my head back and stared straight ahead at the dirt wall, sinking the toes of my sneakers into the soil, then my fingers, lowering myself like I was on a ladder. This is how Brittany had done it and it seemed to work. At the bottom I caught my breath, and turned to her for some confirmation of the difficulty of what we'd just done, a little shared triumph, but she was already looking away down the arroyo. "The machine is this way," she said.

The fog had settled in. It was like walking in a dream, hazy and indistinct. The only sound was the soft crunch of our footsteps in the dirt. At one point Brittany reached back and I could only see her hand, opening and closing, so I took it. I'd never held a girl's hand before. For some reason I felt like I wanted her to know that, I wanted to tell her, but my palm was wet and before I could say anything her hand slipped free and then the fog thinned and a shadow rose up in front of us, tall and wide and gray. We stepped closer and there it was, the bridge across the arroyo, but to me, to us, it was the water machine, its massive metal legs reaching up through the fog.

We stood quietly and every few seconds I could hear a car pass high overhead, a long, low *thrum*, the hollow sound holding and then fading to silence.

Brittany knelt by the machine's leg. "Keep an eye out," she said. "This place is full of guards." She unzipped her backpack and pulled out a pink alarm clock. There were two silver bells on the top, with a little silver hammer standing in between. She set the clock at the base of the leg and then pulled a length of red wire from her backpack. She handed me the end of the wire and motioned for me to carry it around the leg. When I brought the end back to her, she stuck it in her mouth and used her teeth to peel off an inch of the plastic coating, exposing the thin copper threads inside. She wrapped the exposed end around the clock's hammer, twisting it tight.

She stopped then, and held out a hand for silence, though I wasn't making any noise. Then I heard them, too: crunching footsteps approaching from under the machine. I squatted and ran my fingers along the ground, searching for a rock, anything I could use as a weapon, but I found only stiff weeds sprouting from the dirt.

I imagined Denny and Rey and my dad coming through the fog. I couldn't think of anything scarier than them finding us out here, finding these kids so far from home.

"Take my helmet," I said to Brittany, unbuckling the chin strap. "They might think you're one of them."

She looked at me and shook her head and said, "They'd never believe that."

The footsteps came closer. I wanted to run. I hated myself for being scared, wondering what they'd all think of me, Luke and Liam and Brittany with her school clothes and Hello Kitty backpack, waiting bravely with her clock and her wires. I could hear my dad yelling at me to toughen up, his voice shouting over and over in my head. *Are you going to cry now, Frankie? Cry for me you fucking baby. Show me how you cry.* It was his voice, then it was my voice, like when I'd get Curt Lin on the floor of the school bathroom, kicking him, slapping him, squeezing his face in my hand, trying to get that voice out of my head and into his.

Cry for me you fucking baby. Show me how you cry.

Just as I was about to turn and sprint, two shapes appeared in the fog, and I yelled out, a loud roar to blast through the fear. I could imagine the sound blowing apart the fog, the water machine, the entire arroyo, Denny and Rey and their house, my dad on the porch. I was so scared, I just wanted it all to go away.

When I stopped yelling and opened my eyes, Luke and Liam were standing where the shadows had been. Luke had his rifle pointed at me and then he lowered it and said, "Holy shit, I thought you were going to kill us."

Liam stood trembling. His eyes were wet, like he was going

to cry. Brittany had turned to me, too. She looked shocked, as if she now saw me as someone completely different than who she'd thought I was.

Finally she blinked hard, like she was clearing the moment away, and knelt again by the alarm clock, turning it over to reveal a switch on its back.

"Wait," Luke said. "Before we set the detonator, we need to know he can be trusted."

"He gave us the plans," Liam said.

"That's not enough," Luke said. They were all facing me now. "He could have been yelling for help. It could be a trap."

"It's not," I said.

Luke stuck a finger into my chest. "You sounded like you were going to kill us just now," he said. "How do we know that you're not still one of them?"

Brittany stood and stepped toward me, unafraid, looking right up into my eyes. "Give us something else," she said. "More classified information. Tell us something you shouldn't tell anybody."

They all stood, waiting. I didn't know what to say. I didn't want to lie again, but I was afraid that if I told them the truth—the real truth—they'd hate me, they'd be afraid of me. But I didn't want to hold it in anymore, either. I thought that maybe if I told them the truth, then somehow it wouldn't just be mine anymore, I wouldn't be alone with it.

"There's a kid at my school," I said, "named Curt Lin."

I looked at each of them as I spoke.

"Almost every day I hurt him really bad."

"Why?" Liam said.

I shook my head. For a long time no one said anything, but no one looked away, either.

Then Brittany said, "Are you going to keep doing it?"

"I don't know," I said. "I don't know what to do."

We stood like that, watching each other. Finally, Luke cleared his throat and said, "All right. Set it."

Brittany crouched back down next to the alarm clock and clicked the switch on the back. Then she took a deep breath and stood and said, "Go," and Luke started to run and we all followed. I tried to keep them in sight, but all I could see were shadows in the fog, so I followed the shadows, the sounds of their breathing, until one of them dropped to the ground, and then the rest of us dropped, and we all lay in the dirt covering our heads with our arms. There was a hand on my back then, and I reached out a hand and put it on whoever's back was closest, and then the hand on my back squeezed, so I squeezed, and Luke said, "Boom."

Luke led us up the embankment and across the clearing to the line of scraggly trees. The fog was fading, revealing a gauzy sun that seemed to throb along with a headache I could feel starting. I hadn't eaten since that morning, a bowl of cereal. The whole day had passed.

We crossed through the line of cypress and onto the path between the backyards. The kids in the sandbox were gone, so was the couple in their garden. We walked in silence. The boys carried their guns loosely, as if the weapons had lost their weight somewhere back in the arroyo.

On the sidewalk in front of their house we stopped, and Luke stepped up to me. "You've got to go back," he said. "So the guards will still think you're one of them."

I didn't want to play the game anymore. I wanted them just to be the kids on this street who I could visit again the next time I was here. I wanted to tell them more truths, that my dad wasn't an actor, that he'd probably stolen the helmet. That my mom had spent the whole day at a farm stand watching cars come down off the freeway ramp, wondering if they were going to stop.

I didn't say anything, though. Instead, I handed Luke my helmet. He asked how the other guards would know me when I went back, and I said that they'd know me with or without it. He nodded, and held his hand up to his forehead. Liam did the same, then Brittany. I held up my hand and we saluted, and then I turned back down the hill toward the men on the porch.

It was getting dark; a few lights blinked on in the neighboring houses. When I reached the red pickup, Denny and Rey went back inside their house, leaving a string of empty cans across the front yard. My dad and I walked to the bus stop at the corner. He was quiet, and seemed tired. He didn't mention the missing helmet, but waiting at the stop, he asked who I had been playing with, who I knew in this neighborhood. The bus pulled to the curb, its engine thundering. I didn't know how to answer him, if I could say friends, if that would be true. So instead I said rebels, I said soldiers, but the bus's engine was so loud that he didn't hear me. He tilted his head like a dog that didn't quite understand, but before I could repeat myself his hand was on my back, pushing me up onto the bus.

The Plagiarist

Sunrise over the mountains, a thin margin of early light growing slowly above the topmost ridge. Richard stood in the hotel suite's living room, naked under his robe, the air-conditioning raising a pleasurable chill on his skin. A view of the red desert stretched from one set of windows; the high, close wall of mountain filled another. Down below, Palm Springs's flat, orderly arrangement of Spanish tiled rooftops and golf greens spread out in between. He sipped his coffee, coming awake, feeling the rooms below his feet stirring, imagining the movement, all the other suites of actors, producers, the director and screenwriter, the men and women who had retold Richard's story, reshaping it from words on a page to pure action and dialogue, motion and sound. The space buzzed now, he could feel it, the hotel full of his creation, one giant organism with his brain at the top.

He had been to many press junkets, shilling for movie versions of his stories that ranged from direct-to-video cheapies to big budget summer blockbusters. But this one felt different.

It had the same electrical charge of his first junket thirty years before, for the original version of this new film. That day had been all pomp and promise, and this felt like a bookend to that experience, the finishing of a shape that had been left incomplete.

Through the open door he could see the uproar of the bedroom, books and papers scattered across the floor, the bed, the dressers. The edges of a hangover threatened. Richard knew that he should have gone to sleep earlier, but he was working again, finally, and refused to cut off his newfound momentum. He hadn't been able to put together a successful story in years, but the imminent release of this film had sparked something within him. He had spent too long in that black void, unable to create. He wasn't going back again.

A sheet of paper slid beneath the door of his suite: the day's itinerary. He recognized many of the reporters' names from magazines and TV. Heavyweights, most of them. After so much time away, he was finally back in that league.

At the windows he stood for another moment, while the glass and view brightened, his body warming from coffee and sun, the promise of the day.

He wrote his first story when he was five, a two-page tale of an alien invasion of his elementary school. It was praised by his teacher, held up as a model of imagination, vivid detail, memorable characters. He continued writing, and the celebration of his work continued as well. Hailed as a prodigy, he was called onstage at school assemblies, at Santa Clarita civic meetings to read his work. Ideas came easily, as did the words that brought them to life. When he was seven, Richard read a story on a local radio program. At ten, he was invited down to Los Angeles to read on a TV telethon raising money for muscular dystrophy. Two sounds from that evening remained with him: the ringing of phones from off to the side of the stage and the clacking of wooden numbers as the host increased the tote-board totals, unable to move fast enough to keep up with the incoming calls.

He told stories to his classmates; to his father in their pickup on the way to school, before the old man went off to his job handing out brochures and answering tourists' questions at the Visitor's Bureau. But it was Richard's mother who encouraged him the most. Every evening, she came home from her shifts at the diner and sat on the sofa and submerged her feet in a large metal bowl of ice water and asked Richard to tell her a story. These were his favorite moments of the day, sitting beside his mother and creating a story from nothing, from adventures at school, from dreams, fears and worries, and watching her face as she listened, her head back, eyes closed, forehead slowly relaxing, her taut features smoothing out like pond ripples calming, the tension of the day released as he spoke.

Where do they come from? she would ask when he had finished a story. Her eyes still at rest, a soft, slight smile at her lips, and his only answer, the only honest answer, because the world was full of stories, and they came so readily, so easily, was to say, *Everywhere.*

* * *

"How many of your stories have been made into movies?"

"Four," he said. "Well, five. This is a remake, though."

"It still counts." The studio's PR girl sipped her juice, then pressed a napkin to her top lip to clear the thin orange line. They were at breakfast down in the bustling hotel restaurant. The interviews would begin soon.

"And a few for a TV anthology years ago," Richard said.

"I think I remember those."

"You would have been very young."

"My boyfriend streams all those shows," she said. "*The Twilight Zone. Beyond the Limits.*"

The PR girl was dark-haired, athletic, her arms tanned and tight with lean muscle. He stole another glance, dropping his eyes to the glass-topped table, the view below, the short skirt hugging her bare thighs. Only half-worried she would catch him, as he was the subject, she was here for him. Throughout breakfast she'd talked continuously about how much she loved his work, how she'd once performed in a college theater production based on one of his stories. The first time I was ever naked onstage, she'd said. He let his eyes linger.

Angie was her name. Or Annie. He was terrible with names.

"*The Outer Limits,*" Richard corrected, forking a jalapeño loose from his omelette and lifting it to his mouth.

"That one, too," the PR girl said.

Richard caught his upside-down reflection in the concave face of a teaspoon. He adjusted his tie. The look he'd cultivated— the light linen suits; the close shave; hair stacked back in short, sculpted waves—he had found in a 1930s detective magazine, a photo of a writer whose name Richard had long since forgotten. But the image made an impression. The look was so striking, deliberate and polished, that he knew it was worthy of resurrection. The key was the slight rumple to every component—hair always a few days overdue for a trim, suit wrinkled—like he was stepping out of a party even as he was just arriving. The lines around his eyes now, the gray in his hair only amplified the effect. He came across as a man who lived, who engaged in adventures both on and off the page.

The PR girl glanced at her own itinerary, then showed Richard a new name penciled in at the end of the day. "Is that okay?" she asked, tapping a pink fingernail on the name. "Adding this woman in? She's from your alma mater. It's not publicity, exactly, but she said she's been studying your work. I know it's making a long day longer, but—"

"Not a problem," Richard said, feeling the day stretching before him pleasantly, seductively, a woman in bed, limbs reaching.

Andrea. Audra.

"I talk to these academics," he said, finding the PR girl's eyes over the top of the itinerary, "and they know more about my work than I do."

For months, his mother had ignored the stomachaches, the pain that shot up the sides of her body like streaks of lightning. By the time she finally saw a doctor, the cancer had already decimated her liver and was moving quickly, greedily, island-hopping from organ to organ. Most of Richard's eighth grade year was spent in the hospital: sitting beside his mother's bed; haunting the gift shop; drinking Cokes in the cafeteria while his father sat across the table, staring into a Styrofoam coffee cup. One Friday night, when his father had gone home to get some rest, and Richard had stayed to sleep over in the stiff pleather lounger beside his mother's bed, she'd taken his hand and said, *Tell me a story.* Looking at her face, starved and dried nearly to bone, her eyes crusted in the corners, her lips cracking with thirst, he faltered for the first time. Nothing came. Richard was speechless, silent in that room full of ticking machines. Looking back to his mother, he hoped to see that familiar, encouraging smile, but instead he saw fear and desperation. *Tell me one of your stories*, she said again, as if grasping for some saving thread, something to keep her there, with him in that room. But Richard couldn't think of where to start. His mind was an empty space. She squeezed his hand again, and he realized that she was squeezing with every new burst of pain, her face was stricken with it, and so he started telling her a story from a science fiction magazine he had bought down in the gift shop earlier that day. He recounted it slowly, as if he were spinning it from nothing, pure imagination, like he had done for her so many times before. She held his hand all through the story, her grip tightening from blasts of pain but also from the urgent desire to stay with him, and he was aware that the story was keeping her there, her belief that it was coming solely from him, a creation from her own creation. So Richard continued telling the story, and every day after, for all the days remaining, he told more stories from that magazine, from other books and magazines, because in the face of their shared fear he had nothing of his own to offer.

One after another the reporters came, ushered in by the PR girl to sit on the love seat opposite Richard. They shook his hand; they placed phones and recorders on the coffee table. They checked the time. They had fifteen minutes each. They asked what he thought of the movie. He loved the movie. He loved all the movies, even the direct-to-video cheapies. They were loud and garish and magnificent, like funhouse reflections of his work, like wayward children. For some, he had been asked to write the screenplay, or to stretch the story out to a novel-length tie-in. He had declined all the offers, no matter the money. The reporters asked the usual question: Why didn't he write something longer? He gave his usual answer. I think in stories. I think in short, sharp shocks. Over the years it had become the title of more than a few magazine profiles: *Richard Meller's Short, Sharp Shocks*. Richard loved that line. It described his work perfectly, almost as if it had been his own thought, rather than a phrase he had found in a crime story published eighty years before.

He began to disappear. That's what it felt like, after his mother's funeral, when she was gone but the void remained. Richard and his father moved through the house silently, carefully, as if they were avoiding something, some presence that stood between them.

He tried to write but nothing came. His mind remained a blank, the bleeding edge of that surrounding emptiness. He lost himself in pulp magazines, library books, drugstore paperbacks. Fantastic stuff, gaudy and overblown. He was looking to escape the terrible stillness of the house and his memories of the hospital room, his failure there. But every once in a while he came across a sentence, or even just a fragment, a small, tight chain of words that spoke to him, that described the fear and loneliness he had felt in that room, sitting beside his mother's bed, unable to help, to do the one thing she had asked—to hold her there with something of his own.

He wrote those sentences down, and began looking for others that made him feel the same way. He began to realize that these phrases and paragraphs didn't belong where he had found them, that they were in the wrong stories. They belonged together, in his notebook. He could see how one fit into the other, how they locked into place, creating a beautiful rhythm, a fierce fire that spread across the page. He developed a sense of where things were in an old story, where he would find what he needed: characters, scenarios, settings. Alone in his room, from book to magazine and around again he assembled these pieces, painstakingly constructing new stories, recapturing the feeling he'd had before his mother's illness, the wonder and thrill of creation. The world was full of stories, he had told her countless times, and that was finally true again.

Time travel stories, alternate universes, settlers creating new colonies on distant planets. Fantastic scenarios that spoke to something deeper, something true: grief, fear, loss of control, impossible hope. He assembled pieces for school assignments, Kiwanis talent shows, college applications. His stories—and they were *his* stories now—were read again, praised again. They opened doors, freeing him first from that confining memory of his mother's hospital room, then from his father and the silent, suffocating house in Santa Clarita.

Richard stepped through those doors, out of that void, and finally reentered the world.

"Where do you get your ideas?"

Another question he had been asked a thousand times. A film critic with a skunk's white stripe in his hair leaned in from the love seat, waiting for an answer. Richard paused for effect, feigned a searching, introspective look. Something of an actor himself.

"The stories are already inside me. They've always been there."

The critic sat back, nodding, jotting in his notepad.

"My job," Richard said, "is just to let them out."

November, 1968
Dear Mr. Meller,

I read your story "Daylight" in the newest issue of Interstellar Tales, *a maga{ine my husband buys at the news-stand. I had never read an issue before but had finished my*

own magazine with time still remaining on the morning's
chemotherapy treatment.

Richard received his first letter during his sophomore year at college, not long after his first story had been published. It was a generic greeting card, a Monet reproduction printed on the front, *The Waterlily Pond with the Japanese Bridge.* The interior was blank, but held a folded sheet of notepaper, as if the sender realized that her sentiment belonged on its own page, and the drugstore card was simply a wrapper, a vessel for its delivery.

> *I cannot express how I felt about the story, what happened*
> *to me while reading it in my chair in the clinic. Hooked up*
> *to those machines, pumped with drugs, I felt like the woman*
> *in your story, half human, half chemical. Reading her voice,*
> *her thoughts, I felt understood, maybe. Or heard. It's hard to*
> *describe. I'm not a writer.*
>
> *I cut the story out of the magazine and have taken it with*
> *me to every treatment since. Will you write more about her? I*
> *feel that I need to know what happens—if she survives, what*
> *her life is like after.*

Reading the letter, Richard was able to imagine the woman clearly, in the same way he had once been able to imagine characters for stories. He couldn't put words to the feeling, that surprising connection, but she already had, and so he saved the letter. He began to receive others. A housewife who had just discovered that her husband of twenty-five years was cheating on her; a physics professor terrified of leaving his house; a boxer whose childhood friend had just suffered a series of strokes. They had read his stories and understood what he was creating, the void he was circling, those ineffable feelings from back in his mother's hospital room. They understood how Richard had taken those emotions and blown them up to a scale so large that he and his readers could look at them directly, like a safe angle when staring into the sun.

He saved the letters inside a folder on his writing desk. He brought them along to every convention and junket and premiere. Untouched, usually, but present, there if he needed them. When he doubted his ability or methods, he opened one, his eyes running across the familiar handwriting, the lines he'd long since memorized. He began to think of them as his anchor, his foundation. Toward the end of his marriage, when Victoria was nearly frantic with rage, she hadn't threatened to destroy his manuscripts or awards, the movie posters signed by famous actors. It was the folder she threatened, aiming the can of lighter fluid at his precious pages and threatening to squeeze, to strike a match.

Many times over the years, he had tried to write stories on his own again, without his growing collection of magazines and paperbacks. Jolted by guilt, or fear of discovery, like a drunk jumping back on the wagon. He tried after his first collection was published, and he started giving interviews, answering questions. He tried again when Victoria moved into the house in St. Petersburg, the year before their wedding, and Richard feared that she would open some of the dog-eared books and magazines in his sunroom office and recognize characters, lines of dialogue, turns of phrase. And he tried whenever he heard from his father, when he received those infrequent, increasingly disoriented phone calls from California, the old man tearily reminding Richard of how much his mother had loved his stories, how much they had meant to her.

During those times he boxed up his collection, cleared the room and sat at his desk, his notebook open to a blank page. But the page never became less blank, and Richard could feel himself slipping, disappearing back into that void. Months or a year would go by before he was able to claw his way up to working again, reopening those boxes, his books and magazines, finding a first sentence, then the next, finally regaining his sense of himself. Months lost, a year lost, swearing that he would never try again, never go back, slip away, disappear.

It turned out that his fears were unfounded. The questions from interviewers never probed very deeply; the movie people never asked any questions at all. Victoria rarely set foot in the sunroom. She didn't care about his work methods, only the royalty statements, their status at the country club, the flights to the west coast for Hollywood premieres.

Richard was the only one who cared, he was his only judge, and he realized, finally, that no justification was necessary. Did architects mix their own cement, shape their own bricks? Did every painter grind his own pigments? Answering his own questions alone in the sunroom, while Victoria was at tennis, at the salon.

What about jazz musicians, who quoted from one another mercilessly, stealing riffs and chord progressions?

No one calls that theft. We call it art.

So what was this?

"Richard?"

He turned from the window. The PR girl, Amanda, Annie, leaned into the suite's doorway, her face in the frame, mouth pulled low in an apologetic frown.

"I'm sorry," she said. "You've got one more, remember? That grad student. After her, you're done, I promise."

"Let's get a drink then," Richard said, straightening. The void was always threatening; always needed to be held at bay. "Just the two of us," he said. "In celebration of a hard day's work."

The PR girl nodded, her lips rising in a satisfying smile, pulling him back, just a step or two, from the edge.

"I'd like to show you some research my group has been working on."

The grad student's name was Lydia. Richard had no problem remembering her name, which struck him as odd, as most everything else about her was unremarkable. She was the same age as the PR girl, but with pallid, unsunned skin and unfashionable glasses that matched her flat brown hair. A woman who spent her time indoors, he thought, staring at screens. She seemed nervous, touching her index finger to the ball of her nose before asking a question, as if it were a button that needed to be pushed before she could speak.

She had the usual inquiries—Why only short stories? Where do you get your ideas?—and Richard gave his usual answers. Her reactions to his responses were flat like her coloring. She seemed uninterested in his answers; it was as if these questions were merely a formality.

But now, opening her laptop, she straightened a bit. Her face and body lifted, infused with a new energy. This was what she had been waiting for. She wanted to show her work. She wanted his advice, his approval.

Lydia paused, the laptop screen still obscured. "I want you to know," she said, "that I've read your work my whole life. My father died when I was six, and I became a reader to escape."

She paused for a moment, clearly uncomfortable. She blinked and touched the tip of her nose again, which seemed to help her continue.

"At least, I thought that's why I read. But your stories—these stories—weren't just an escape. They seemed like an echo of my own thoughts, my feelings. I've carried them with me ever since."

Richard sat forward on the sofa. There was something about her—her intelligence, her suddenly exposed vulnerability—that made him want to tell her about his mother, show her the folder of letters. Strange, he thought—it was not so much a desire for admiration, and there was no physical desire here on his part. He simply wanted her to know. She seemed like another reader who might understand.

"Anyway," she said, embarrassed, flushing with the first show of color. "My work."

"Of course," Richard said, smiling, trying to put her back at ease. "Show me."

Richard's father had spent the last years of his life in a nursing home just north of Santa Clarita, slipping deeper and deeper into a dementia that riddled his memory, his sense of time and actuality. Whenever Richard visited, his father rattled off long strings of detailed memories that had never happened, but Richard felt it was his job to confirm that they had, that he remembered those things, too. This seemed to make his father happy, or at least content. His father's real memories were gone, or buried. He no longer mentioned Richard's mother, or their lives together in the house in Santa Clarita, the stories Richard had once told on their drives to school. Instead, his father recounted new names, places, events, all in the greatest detail, with the greatest emotion, his eyes wet with remembrance.

Richard hadn't spoken at his mother's funeral. He was too young, too grief-stricken. But two years ago, when his father finally succumbed, Richard felt the need to memorialize the man with whom he'd spent those empty years after his mother's death. He had been unable to understand his father then, his silence, his inward turn, and over the following decades their relationship remained strained and distant. But witnessing his father's slow loss of engagement with reality had reminded Richard of his own loss, that first tumble into the void, and this evoked such a feeling of sympathy, of admiration for the stoic courage the old man had displayed in the face of his wife's death, his perseverance in raising his son alone, that Richard was driven to write a memorial, a speech that would not only recall his father's best qualities, but that would help make sense of his newfound appreciation for the man, untangling the silent mysteries of those years they had spent alone together.

For two days he worked at his desk, in his notebook, ignoring calls from friends, his publisher, Victoria's lawyer. But on the morning before the service, his notebook pages were still blank. Finally he capitulated, and spent the remainder of the day at the library's microfiche machine, reading through a century's worth of obituaries, hastily crafting his own from the pieces that seemed most authentic and apt. At the service, he stood at the lectern and delivered a eulogy that left most of the mourners in tears. But as he shook hands and accepted condolences and commendations his secret failure grew within him, a shadow-self Richard could feel in every nerve and muscle, pulling him back into the void.

He had floated there these last two years, gasping in the dark. It was the announcement of the new movie that had pulled him out, the first billboards and TV teasers, like a voice, his own voice remembered, finally calling him back.

"It's an information retrieval system," Lydia said. "Lines of code that will eventually read everything there is to read."

Richard looked at the spreadsheet displayed on Lydia's laptop. It made no sense. The screen was filled with rows and columns of what looked like snippets of phrases, clauses, lines of dialogue.

"I'm sorry," he said, looking up from the screen. "But what does this have to do with my work?"

"The system catalogs and then cross-references," she said.

"Cross-references what?"

"Duplications," she said. "Repetitions."

This had been a mistake. Letting his vanity get the better of him, he'd probably wasted so much time that his drink with the PR girl wouldn't come to pass. But maybe if he excused himself now, before Lydia went any further, he could still salvage some of the—

"Over the course of your career you've written seventy-seven stories," Lydia said. "And every one contains material copied directly from other sources."

Richard felt the air-conditioning on his skin again, working its way below the fabric of his shirt, prickling the hairs on his arms, the back of his neck. He tried to speak but his throat had dried shut.

"In many of them," Lydia said, "the percentages were the highest my research team has ever seen. Seventy-five, eighty percent, taken directly from other novels and stories, all previously out of print."

Richard looked away from Lydia, down to her recorder, the little black box on the coffee table. He imagined her voice passing her lips and then pausing in the room for him to hear, to process, before traveling into the recorder's microphone, its flash drive, the entire works no bigger than a thumbprint, where her voice would be coded, where it would remain, along with his, for all to hear, forever after.

He wanted to run, to stand and flee the room, but he stayed seated on the couch. Her voice, the black box, like magnets.

All that week before the junket, he'd been caught in the first swells of the new story, the rush of inspiration he feared he would never feel again. He had spent rich, glorious hours in the musty stacks of antiquarian bookshops, the basements of far-flung library branches, the open-air stalls of flea markets and swap meets. Some of the books he found hadn't been borrowed since the Ford administration, were inscribed to friends and lovers during World War II or Korea. Many bore unidentifiable stains on the covers, carried silverfish in their latter chapters. All had been forgotten, discarded, sitting on shelves now, in soft piles, damp boxes, waiting.

He had filled an extra suitcase with his discoveries, gladly paying the weight surcharge before boarding the plane to Palm Springs. On the flight, he was already reassembling the sentences he had found. He could see them as if they were still on their original pages, their positions within paragraphs, the snug families where they had sat for half a century or longer. Then he could see their removal, the blank spot they left, and their combination with other sentences from other stories on a fresh page, clean and white. Arriving at the hotel he'd gone straight up to his suite, ordered a bottle and opened his suitcases and locked the doors, assembling the puzzle in his notebook, moving from books to magazines and around again, circling the bedroom, a glass of rye in his hand, a conductor signaling his players, combining the disparate lost sounds into a new piece, cutting, adding, rearranging until it felt right, settling into place, as if this was the way it always should have been, as if this was the story as it was meant to be told.

Finally, he met her eyes. There was more color in them than he had originally thought, lavender highlights that caught the last of the day's sun. Lydia held them there for a moment, staring back, then dropped her gaze to the laptop.

"This passage from your story 'Thalassa' is identical to this passage from 'The Cave of Memory' by H. H. Burden," Lydia said, "published in 1937. Everything except the character names, which came from another story published a year later."

She moved her cursor around the screen, dragging a highlight across the familiar sentences.

"They let you in here," Richard said. "The PR girl—Annie, Abigail—"

"Audrey," Lydia said. "I told her I was a reader, that I'd devoted my work to yours. I told her the truth."

He looked away again. The late afternoon sun sent a low slant of light across the carpeting, up the side of the couch. Richard moved his fingertips into its path, but felt none of its warmth on his skin.

"At first I thought that there must be something wrong with the program," she said. "I thought that *I* was wrong."

He stood. He didn't know why he was standing. To scare or dismiss her? To run?

"But it turns out I'd been lied to. All of us"—she gestured to the room, the rooms beyond, below—"have been lied to."

He needed to say something, to explain himself. He needed to tell her about the telethon, his first trip to Los Angeles, standing onstage, telling a story, the ringing phones off to the side, the clacking of the tote-board total behind him.

"We're going public with our research tomorrow," Lydia said. "But I wanted to give you an opportunity to respond before publication."

He needed to tell her about the letters, the connection they proved, what they meant to him.

She turned the laptop back around, positioned her hands over the keys, thin fingers bent, ready to type.

He needed to tell her about his mother's hospital room, her hand in his, the void. But the words wouldn't come. Such a familiar feeling. Instead he said, "You're going to take all of this away," understanding as soon as the words left his mouth that she thought he meant the suite, the movie, the PR girl.

Lydia looked back down at her screen.

"It was never yours to begin with," she said.

After Lydia had left the suite, Richard stood alone at the windows. It seemed as if he could feel the news traveling through the building below him, down its spine like a lit fuse, into the other suites of actors, producers, the director and screenwriter. The hotel was a charged weapon now, ready to detonate. He could imagine it collapsing, coming down around him. He could imagine what it would feel like to be trapped, pinned beneath.

He left his books, his notebook, the folder of letters in the bedroom and walked from the hotel, into the night world of the desert city, windows bright with electric light, lawns glittering with stolen water. He was never able to imagine anything further of his stories after he'd finished them, but walking alone along the broad boulevards and even sidewalks, the level fabrication of the place, he could picture what the city might be like on the desert planet of his story, of their movies. He was walking through it now; it was all around him.

After a while he lay down on a grassy berm beside a cinder-block wall. He was tired in a way he'd never felt before. Closing his eyes, he could hear the wind, a banshee wail rushing down from the mountains. In his dream he was in a medical clinic, was a woman sitting in a medical clinic, a room full of ticking machines. His body, her body, had turned murderous, and so they were pumping her full of poison. She could feel it flooding her system, killing off the old version of herself. She was turning into something new now, half-human, half-chemical, her body bright and dark with it, nearly bursting with fear and hope.

In the first pale light of day he walked to a diner at the edge of the city. A bell over the door rang as he entered. It was a newer place, or had been restored from an older place. The paint was fresh, the vinyl on the booths shiny and smooth. He sat on a stool at the counter. After a while a waitress joined him from the other side. She was tall, middle-aged, with an unsteady gait, toddling a little as she moved from station to station. A muscle issue maybe, or an old injury. He ordered coffee and sat and drank, not realizing that the waitress was still there, speaking to him. She said he looked like he'd had a hell of a night.

The coffee had sloshed a little when she'd poured, and he looked down to the counter, the dark liquid line spreading slowly, diverted by the nicks and chips in the Formica.

"This is original," he said, tapping the counter. The waitress nodded, but his thoughts were still down in the cracks and divots, their feel on his fingertips, the same as the counter in his mother's diner back in Santa Clarita where he had spent so many afternoons, perched on a stool, telling her stories during the lull before the dinner rush. This crack is a mighty river, navigated by brave explorers. This divot is a volcano, hiding a great secret, a monster of enormous power and size.

The waitress asked his name. There in the void he didn't know where the name came from, it was just there suddenly, and so he grabbed it, said it as if it were his own, as if it were true, and then the waitress nodded, accepting, and it was true. She asked where he was from, and he answered with the first city that came into his head, and now there was weight behind the name: a place, a history, the beginnings of a life. The waitress refilled his coffee and continued asking questions, so he continued answering, reaching, climbing, telling her the story as it came.

Colnago Super

I always thought of stealing as an art. By that I mean that when I was looking for something, or when I was taking it, the world transformed, it became a different place, in the same way, I think, as when people talk about how playing music or making a painting takes them somewhere else, at least for a little while.

The bike was a Raleigh Gran Sport, gold with white trim, a '74 or '75, only a couple of years old. Newly washed, shining, its frame caught the sun, glinting like the rings on the fingers of the women window-shopping along Beverly Boulevard. The Raleigh was cable-locked to a parking meter outside of a coffee shop, and the tables outside the shop were empty, unoccupied in the unseasonable heat, so the bike stood there alone, unwatched.

I pedaled a few streets up and stashed my Schwinn behind a gas station Dumpster. I always rode my own bike while I worked. I didn't think that a teenage girl on a bicycle would be suspected of stealing another. So far, I'd been right. The Schwinn was a battered men's Sprint that I'd taken a year earlier and had since painted sky blue. Light and fast and unremarkable, it was a bike no one in their right mind would bother to steal, which is exactly why I'd stolen it. I knew that whenever I returned, I'd find the Schwinn right where I'd left it.

Walking back toward Beverly, I started to sweat, both from the heat and the anticipation, waiting for the change that came when I was in motion, pointing myself toward a bike. I was always afraid that it wouldn't happen—that this might be the time where nothing changed. Turning the corner, though, I felt the shift. Colors became brighter—the sapphire reds and chromium blues of passing cars, women's skirts in citrusy yellows and greens, the teal shine of office building windows reflecting the whitened sky. Sounds grew clearer and more distinct. I could hear every horn honk and bus engine and barking dog. The shoppers on the sidewalk began to move in blurry slow-motion, until the only thing in focus was the golden bike at the end of the block.

This was my sign, my green light. I didn't believe in religion or magic; I was only superstitious in that moment. Seeing that a bike I'd chosen was still there as I approached was the only time I could believe there were signals hidden in the world, and that this was one I had deciphered. Once I felt that signal, I never left a bike. If I left it and came back, I knew it would be gone. The signal put me in motion. There was no second-guessing, no turning back. All that was left were the mechanics—coming up on the Raleigh and pulling my bump key and springing the lock, letting its cord slither loose, then swinging my leg over the seat and standing, just for a moment, my sneakers on the pedals, our bodies together in perfect balance. No one on the sidewalk paid any attention.

Perched on the Raleigh, the sound and color spiked, a crescendo, that note shivering up from the soles of my feet to the crown of my head. I took a breath, at the center of the secret, heightened world, then I pushed the crank and pedaled away.

The feeling didn't last. It never did. By the time I reached the impound lot in Highland Park, the world had faded, and I was drained, achy, hungry. Donald, the guy who worked at the lot, would only give me fifteen bucks for the Raleigh. He told me that he couldn't get more than twenty or twenty-five for it resale, which was bullshit by about half, but Donald was the only fence I knew, so I didn't have much going in the way of leverage.

I took the bus back to Beverly, getting off a block away from the coffee shop. The Schwinn was right where I'd left it. I rode back home to Atwater, and by the time I reached the entrance to the trailer park, even the last little jolt of the feeling was gone. The world was just the world again, slow-burning, dulled, smoggy with muted yellows and browns.

Inside our trailer, I found my father in his wheelchair watching the news. There was a nearly empty bottle of vodka in his lap, and a little had spilled—or something had spilled—across the thigh of his pajama pants. But there were no other bottles or cans in the immediate vicinity, and Gary seemed fairly lucid, rolling his eyes toward me as I stepped up into the trailer and then raising his eyebrows by way of a greeting.

Gary was a blackout drunk before he was diagnosed with MS, but once he'd found out that the tremors and weakness and stumbling falls weren't just caused by drinking, he took that as his own kind of sign, a green light to go all out. He'd finish a fifth of vodka before I'd finished breakfast. At the end of the day during a particularly bad stretch I'd find a grocery bag full of empties out on the trailer's front step and Gary slumped inside in his chair. Sometimes he'd thrown up on himself, or wet his pajama pants, and I had to clean him up or wheel him to the shower to rinse him off. He was heavy and tall, but I was tall, too, like him, and my legs were so strong from riding that I was able to get him out of the chair and into the tub. I tried to keep my eyes on the spraying water, away from all the flesh and hair. Once he had passed out again in his chair, I'd shower alone, with the water as hot and hard as I could make it, as if I could hose the entire past half hour off of me, scrub it loose, wash it down the drain.

Medi-Cal scheduled a nurse every Monday morning, and sometimes she showed up and took care of everything. But even then there were still six other days in the week.

"Ellie," he said. His voice tired and heavy with booze. He shifted his eyes back to the TV. "Another kid," he said. "They got another one."

That summer, there were kidnappings all along the east side of the city. Poorer kids, mostly, taken from parks and playgrounds. One little boy was even taken from the children's section of the library in El Sereno. There were so many stories and rumors swirling, it was impossible to tell what was real, who'd

heard what on the news versus what they'd heard from somebody who knew somebody who knew somebody else. But it
didn't really matter. Just the idea was enough to create a blanket
of fear over the neighborhood. Just the possibility, that threat in
the air.

The news switched to a commercial. Gary rolled his eyes to
mine. "They showed his picture on TV," he said. "The kid they
took. I thought I recognized him, but I didn't."

I wheeled him into the kitchen, backing his chair to the sink to
dye his hair. This was something he insisted on, every month or
so, though he never left the trailer anymore. He'd been a record
producer in the '60s, a handsome man about town, and that look
was something he wanted to maintain, even though I was terrible
at coloring his hair and the cheap dye we used looked like shoe
polish: too glossy, too black. Little kids in the trailer park were
terrified of him; they'd dare each other to run up to our windows and peek in to get a glimpse. Propped in his chair with his
hair freshly dyed, he looked like a stiffened Dracula, long limbs
splayed at odd angles, face twitching and spasming into violent
frowns and grimaces. Sometimes I walked into the trailer and felt
that same fear, like there was something terrible inside of him,
trying to claw its way out.

I pulled on the dye kit's thin plastic gloves, shook the little
bottle of Sable #5. Gary closed his eyes, listening to the familiar
sounds of the ritual.

"That kid from the front of the park was looking in the window again," he said. "Marvin?"

"Martín. You didn't yell at him, did you?"

"Doesn't he have parents?"

"They work."

"Ten years from now he'll be holding up a liquor store. Boosting cars. He's gonna be stuck here his whole life."

Tilting his head back into the sink, I ran my hands through the water, waiting for it to warm, and then through his hair, which was dry and brittle from the years of dye. He kept his eyes closed and told me what he always told me when he was sober, or sober enough: that I should go, I should leave, that one day when he was bad off I should walk out the door and never look back.

I adjusted the gloves and said what I always said:

"If I go, who'd do all this stuff? Who'd take care of you?"

He shook his head, dismissing the questions. I started combing the dye into his hair.

"When you go," he said, "just go. No goodbyes. That's how you do it. That's how it's done. One day you're here, and the next—"

He struggled to lift his hand from the arm of the wheelchair, allowing the movement to finish his thought, raising his fingers a little, as if letting something float free.

When I was younger, I stole anything I could get my hands on. Candy, cigarettes, Bowie and Lou Reed 45s, paperback books. Whenever things got to be too much with my father, I'd get out of the trailer and head to a store or magazine stand. The stuff I took wasn't important; it was the release I felt during the theft, like I'd made a crack in my life, opened a little hole in the way things were supposed to be.

I was thirteen the first time I saw a bike in that way. I'd had the same flea market Huffy forever. It had gotten so small that I looked like a clown riding around on it, or one of those Shriners with their overlarge bodies on tiny bikes. I didn't really care—the Huffy was just a way to get away from Gary and the park. I rode it to school, or out with my friends, or to the Sears on Santa Monica Boulevard or the liquor store on Brand to take something. But then I saw the man riding the Bertin up Glendale Avenue. Back then, I didn't know it was a Bertin. I didn't know anything about bikes, but I knew that I'd never seen anything like it, so thin and light, like a blade cutting through the air. It was a shiny caramel brown, and I felt like I could almost taste that color, its sweetness on my tongue. I'd stolen a lot of things, but I don't think I'd ever really wanted anything until I saw that bike.

I followed, pedaling furiously on my ridiculous little Huffy. It was hard to keep up. Riding the Bertin appeared effortless to the man; he seemed weightless. Finally, he pulled into a gas station and set the Bertin carefully against the outside wall and jogged in to get something. I knew he'd be back out in a second, he hadn't even locked the bike, but I also knew what I had to do. A green light flashed somewhere in the back of my brain. I ditched the Huffy in the parking lot and ran the rest of the way. Clumsy, obvious, desperate, I climbed on top of the Bertin. I was tall even then, but the bike was still too big, and I had to stretch for the pedals and handlebars. Fumbling, I finally found my grip, my footing. I pushed away from the wall and that's when it hit me, that first time, standing in perfect balance. Everything came into clear, bright focus, my body and the bike's body sharing the same electric charge. Then I heard the man shout and I pedaled out from the gas station.

I'd never gone so fast. It was like flying, what I always imagined flying would be like. I could hear the man shouting, but I knew he'd never catch me, that no one would ever catch me. The wind in my face, in my hair. I felt like if I lifted my hands from the grips I would keep rising, floating away. How could anyone catch me when I felt like that?

I started selling the bikes and saving the money, not really knowing what it was for, or adding up toward. But a few months before that bicentennial summer, the summer of the kidnappings, the answer came to me at a little bike shop on Venice Boulevard. I was buying some grip tape and waiting for the guy behind the counter to make change, when I looked up at the wall behind him and saw the map. Mounted high on a pegboard, between posters of high-end Italian models, Tommasinis and Colnagos, was a wide spread of cross-country bike routes, what seemed like hundreds of multicolored lines radiating out from L.A. in every direction, stretching up into Canada, out to Maine, down to Florida. I stood there long after I had my change, tracing the routes with my eyes, imagining myself along each path, who I might meet or become at different points along those lines, what I would do when I finally reached the water at each color's end.

I started looking for higher-end models to steal, Masis or

Wizards or Weigles. Donald would pay thirty or forty bucks for one of those in good shape. There were bikes everywhere—people were still spooked by the gas prices during the oil embargo a few years before, the endless lines and fistfights at the pumps. Most of what I saw was department store crap, but I kept looking for something great, a big score. I counted the money I kept hidden in a slit in my mattress, dreaming of the map, calculating how close I was to adding up enough fifteen- or twenty-dollar sales to buy a bike that could make that trip, one fast and light and strong enough to take me along one of those lines.

After dyeing Gary's hair, I wheeled him back out into the living room, where he fell asleep in his chair, snoring to beat the band, his still-wet head covered with a shower cap. I was scrubbing the last of the dye out of the sink when there was a knock at the door. I opened it to find Mrs. Romero—Martín's mother. She smiled, or, actually, she was already smiling when I opened the door, standing on the single wooden step in the glare of our trailer's outdoor bulb. She knew my name. She said, Hello, Ellie. She had a pretty thick accent, but her voice was gentle, musical almost. She was short, soft-featured, with light freckles across her nose. She continued smiling as she spoke. I'm sorry to bother you, she said, and I thought she was going to say something about my father, that my father had scared Martín earlier when he had peeked in the window, and I was just about to cut her off and apologize, but then she said, Do you have plans tomorrow?

I said that I didn't, or maybe I just shook my head. I was

worried that she would look past me and see the vodka bottle in the living room, my father in his chair with the shower cap. She seemed so sweet and this would not be a sweet thing to see.

She was still wearing her work uniform, navy-blue pants and a matching shirt with the supermarket logo across one heavy breast. She and Mr. Romero worked at the same store in Hollywood. I knew this because once, a few years before, I saw them both in that market, in a little back hallway by the deli that led to the restrooms. They were standing close together, on a break maybe, and Mr. Romero was eating a powdered doughnut and saying something with his mouth full and Mrs. Romero was laughing so hard and so quietly that it looked like she was crying. I had just shoved about fifteen packs of gum in my pockets, so as soon as I saw them I turned the other way and hustled out of the store.

Standing on the trailer's step, still smiling, she asked if I would be interested in babysitting Martín the next day. At first, I didn't know how to answer. I'd never babysat for anyone. There were a million little kids in the trailer park, but no one had ever asked me before. Maybe they were afraid of Gary, or maybe they just didn't trust me. People in the park kept to themselves mostly, kept their mouths shut, but everybody had eyes, they knew that I didn't really hang out with the other kids my age, kicking around the flagpole after dark, laughing and smoking; they all saw me with a new bike every few days, and have to have wondered where those bikes came from, where they went.

Mrs. Romero's eyes stayed with mine. She didn't try to look past me into the trailer. Either what was behind me didn't matter to her or she was being polite. I appreciated it, whichever it was, and I liked the memory of her laughing in the supermarket hallway, tears in her eyes, Mr. Romero's powdered lips, so I said yes, I'd be happy to babysit Martín.

The next morning, I got up early and walked to the Romeros' trailer. It was already blisteringly hot, the sky bright white, the asphalt shimmering with little wavy pools of mirage. Mr. and Mrs. Romero met me at the door. They were both wearing their uniforms. Martín was back at the kitchen table, eating some Kix, his bowl piled high with little golden balls. Mrs. Romero gave me five bucks, which was more than she said she'd pay the night before, and told me to use the rest of the money to take Martín to a movie. Get out of the heat, she said, still smiling. I wanted to press my face to that smile, feel its shape on my cheek, my neck.

After they left and Martín finished his cereal, we took the bus up to a theater in Glendale. Martín was five; he'd just finished kindergarten. He told me all about it on the ride. It sounded like he had some kind of little kid crush on his teacher, who he said was secretly a princess, and that he knew this because of how her hair smelled when she hugged the kids goodbye at the end of the day. Strawberries, he said, and then he leaned over in his seat and pushed his face into my hair and inhaled. When he sat back I asked him what my hair smelled like and he said, Not strawberries.

The movie was Martín's choice, a science fiction thing he'd seen commercials for on TV. I didn't care much for movies, I didn't like to sit still for that long, but Martín was completely absorbed by it. I spent most of the time watching him. He leaned forward in the seat beside me, his little hand grabbing the armrest or my wrist, eyes wide, his face bright with the light bouncing back from the screen. With every explosion or shout or laser blast he jumped, gripping my arm tighter. At one point, I leaned over and asked him if he was scared and he nodded and so I asked him if he wanted to leave and he turned to me for the first time since the movie started and looked at me like I was crazy. He turned back to the screen but didn't let go of my arm.

After the movie we went to the park across the street. I chased Martín around the playground and bought a couple of ice cream cones with some more of the money Mrs. Romero had given me. Riding the bus home, I wondered if babysitting Martín might become a steady job. It wouldn't bring in as much as selling bikes to Donald, but I liked spending the day with Martín. He was a smart kid, and I liked his stories about kindergarten, his weird questions about things that seemed obvious at first but ended up being pretty hard to answer. Like, How long would it take to walk home from this park? Like, Where's *your* mom, Ellie?

But the day after Martín and I had gone to the movies, his grandmother came out to the park to take care of him. It was cheaper, Mr. Romero told me, when I saw him carrying out his garbage. He seemed apologetic, a little embarrassed. And also, he said, my wife's mother needs someplace to live.

Then I only saw Martín in the early mornings, when I was going out on my bike. Passing the front window of the Romeros' trailer, I could see the back of his head there, his thick brown curls in front of the cartoons on TV.

"Ellie," Gary said. "So quiet." He stared at me from his chair, swallowing hard, trying to get his throat to work enough to continue speaking. It was Friday night, a week after Martín and I saw the movie. I was sprawled on our sofa reading a bike magazine. I had a nearly new Dawes Galaxy stashed out in the toolshed and wanted to be armed with some pricing information when I brought it over to Donald the next morning.

Gary cleared his throat again, then gave up and tilted his head in the direction of the wall of metal shelving at the back of the trailer. That's where he stored his records, hundreds of them, lined up neatly in rows I tried to keep free of cobwebs and dust. The Rolling Stones, Janis Joplin, The Shirelles, The Chiffons. I knew what he wanted. I walked to the shelves and found the LP, pulled it from its jacket and plastic sleeve. On the cover was a singer named Martha Fox. She had a strong, lean face, rich brown skin, dark eyes. She was holding a microphone to her lips, staring at the camera, her expression somewhere between a smirk and a snarl. The record was called *Martha Fox and the Tick-Tocks*. My father had produced it many years ago at a studio in Hollywood. His name was listed on the back cover credits. My mother's name was there, too. She was one of the Tick-Tocks, Martha Fox's backup singers, the only white girl in the group.

I carried the record to the turntable and switched on the receiver. The machine warmed up slowly with a low, velvety hum. I lowered the needle onto the record, and after the first crackles and pops the music began, brash and brassy, Martha Fox's voice full of gravel and attitude. My father listened with his eyes closed, and when the Tick-Tocks sang out in the background, he lifted his eyebrows, the smallest gesture, then cleared his throat and said, "There. Do you hear her?"

I told him that I did, though no matter how many times I listened to that record, I was never able to pick out which voice was hers.

"You don't look like her," he said. His eyes were open now, looking at me, and then they glazed, retreating, remembering. He had stopped swallowing so hard. His voice came easier now; music always seemed to settle him.

"Isn't that strange?" he said. "She was such a beautiful girl. You look more like me."

Later in the bedroom, I stood in front of my mirror and looked at my face, the large features I shared with him, the long range of whiteheads along my cheeks and chin that would one day leave a field of shallow round scars, just like his. I'd only ever seen my mother a few times that I could remember, when an emaciated and strung-out bottle blonde showed up at the trailer asking my father for money. He'd always sent me into the bedroom, where I watched through a crack in the door, staring at the woman, her body bent in desperate need. I tried to see something, anything in her skeletal face, in her posture, that spoke to something in me, that tied us together, some call-and-response like the voices on the record, a shared sound.

I pulled off my T-shirt, my sweatpants. There were scars across the undersides of my forearms, along the muscles of my calves, my inner thighs. Short brown lines, an inch or so long, raised a bit on the skin. Little speed bumps. Before I started taking bikes, I had a few years where I'd take Gary's razor and after I'd shaved his face at the kitchen sink I'd lock myself in the bathroom and pull the blade across my own skin, harder than on his, until I felt the pop and the bite and a little space opened, quickly flooding with blood. Two years, maybe, or three. It always scared the hell out of me, and maybe that's why I did it, because the fear made me lightheaded but awake, apart, like I'd found a place no one else had discovered. When I started taking bikes, I cooled it with the razor. It didn't seem necessary anymore. I realized then that there were other ways to step outside of myself.

It was only when I looked at the scars that I saw any similarity with my mother. That crippled woman, eaten away by need. It was in those moments—when my father played the record out in the trailer, when I imagined I could hear her voice—that it seemed like this image in the mirror was someone she might understand.

A flurry of insistent knocking brought me back out in my pajamas. I padded past Gary, asleep now in his chair, and opened the door to find Mr. and Mrs. Romero and Martín's grandmother standing together on the step. It was the first time I'd seen Martín's grandmother up close. A small woman with a gold-capped overbite, she worked her hands together furiously, as if trying to rub the skin from one to the other. Mrs. Romero wasn't smiling this time, and she looked past me into the trailer, her eyes searching the living room, the kitchen beyond. Before I could ask what was wrong, she started speaking in a hurried jumble of English and Spanish, asking if I had seen Martín. No, I said, but before I could say more, before I could ask what was wrong, she was talking again, pleading. Please, Ellie, she said, tell me that you know where he is. *Que has visto mi hijo.* Please tell me *que está seguro, mi Martín.* Please tell me he's safe.

The next morning, the trailer park was swarming with cops. I worried about Martín but was also freaking out that the cops would poke around in the shed and find the Galaxy I'd parked in there. I started to feel so sick and guilty that after an hour or so I just marched out of our trailer, through the squad cars and worried neighbors, straight to the shed. I climbed onto the Galaxy and rode back through the cops like I owned the thing.

I should have taken the bike straight to Donald, but instead I circled the neighborhood looking for Martín. I rode up Brand Boulevard peering into storefront windows; I rode through the side streets behind the library, the nicer houses with their sloping green lawns, bicentennial flags waving from front porches. I rode along the top of the river's cement wall, looking down into the dry bed, shouting his name. It was a stupid risk, riding that bike with so many cops around. I kept waiting to hear the chirp of a siren coming up behind me.

Finally, I rode out to Highland Park. Donald gave me fifteen bucks for the bike. I didn't even argue, just took the bus back to where I'd stashed my Schwinn and rode back to Atwater. It was evening by then, the sky dimming red above the tree line. Martín still wasn't home. Word had spread while I was away, though, and as I rode back through the neighborhood I could hear other voices on other streets, different layers of distance and volume in the gathering dark, *Martín, Martín,* like echoes of my own voice calling his name.

The story was that Martín had been playing at the park by the elementary school with a few of his friends. There was some sort of disagreement over a toy, and Martín stormed away to the other end of the playground, alone. His grandmother was supposed to be watching the boys, but it was the heat of the day and she'd dozed off sitting beneath one of the school's shady oaks.

Afterward, the other boys remembered a fat white man walking on the other side of the playground fence. They remembered a skinny black man rummaging through the garbage cans. They remembered two women in a yellow van, the same yellow van that had been spotted at the scene of other abductions that summer.

At first, none of the boys remembered seeing Martín with any of the possible suspects. When pressed by their parents or the police, though, their memories began to change. Some said that they could clearly recall Martín walking with the fat white man on the other side of the fence. Some saw him with the skinny black man. Eduardo Lopez, the oldest of the boys, a second grader, was the one who remembered the women and the van. He said he saw

Martín lured into the back with a handful of candy. Jolly Ranchers, he said, red and yellow and green.

Flyers went up around the neighborhood, stapled to telephone poles and taped to stop signs, showing a black-and-white copy of Martín's kindergarten photo and descriptions of the women and the van. Martín's parents went door-to-door in the park, and then out into the surrounding neighborhood, then out into the next. They were joined by other adults who could get off work, or older kids who didn't have summer jobs. I spent those first few days riding in wider and wider rings from the park, pedaling up behind apartments and into vacant lots, calling for Martín, looking for the van. Every night when I returned home, I would find Martín's grandmother, still in her housedress, her apron, walking and wringing her hands, calling his name in her high, unsteady voice like some kind of ghost, haunting the dark lanes between trailers. In bed I'd stick my fingers in my ears, or turn up my clock radio to drown out that sound, thinking that this wouldn't have happened if I had been with him, if I had still been babysitting. I never would have fallen asleep, I thought. I never would have let him out of my sight.

As the week went on, fewer cops showed up. That next Friday morning, when I looked out the trailer's front window, there wasn't a single squad car parked outside. Gary rolled up beside me and looked out and said that the police had moved on, that there were other problems in the city. There was only so long, he said, that everyone would come around looking for the same little brown boy.

* * *

The next day I rode around Glendale, looking for Martín, asking everyone I passed if they'd seen a boy like him, if they'd seen the van. By late afternoon I was fried by the heat and the empty stares. I found myself back at the movie theater, where Martín and I had gone just two weeks before. I bought a ticket and sat alone in the middle of all the empty seats. There was one part of the movie that had stuck with me, one sequence that I remembered as I rode around calling his name. I wasn't exactly sure why, but I wanted to see it again.

It was one of the final scenes, a chase through the long, branching corridors of a vast high-tech facility, a water-making plant on a desert planet. The plant had been sabotaged, flooding with all of the water it had created. The wife of the movie's hero was lost inside. Hearing the first rush of water, she starts to run. The movie's perspective shifts then, to the action seen through her eyes. The movement of the camera—of the woman—is jerky and panicked. She gathers speed, and the walls on either side with their looping wires and blinking lights begin to blur. The sound of the flood grows louder, and when she passes connecting corridors she can see walls of water surging from each side, crashing behind as she runs past. She turns her head this way and that. The camera frame begins to rattle from the speed. The synthesizer music and the sound of the woman's breathing are uncomfortably loud. She runs and runs, the image jumping even more violently, and for a moment it feels like the entire theater will shake apart, but then there's a light, the flat orange sunlight of the alien planet, a square of it growing in the distance, an open doorway getting closer as the woman rushes toward it. Suddenly there's another, smaller figure ahead in the corridor, and I remembered then that I had forgotten that part, that the woman's son was lost there, too. All she can see is the top of his head, his dark curly hair bobbing up in the frame, but she's able to grab him as she runs by. The camera is shaking so violently that the doorway becomes abstract, just shape and color growing to fill the frame. That warm orange light covers the screen, the theater, my face and hands, spreading across my skin, filling my body. Through the doorway, she sees an escape pod gleaming in the distance. She needs to reach it, but the water's here now, there's only time for a single breath. She takes it, and I take it, and she makes one final push and then they're out, free of the corridor, into the open air of the alien planet. The scene cuts outside then, the woman falling to the ground on top of her son, covering him as the water bursts from the doorway like a wild animal, arcing over the two bodies pressed low into the sand. She's gone for a moment, they're both lost below, and then she bursts through to the surface, gasping, still holding her son, swimming now toward the pod.

I had thought it was the thrill of the chase that had stuck with me, like riding a bike down the Cahuenga Pass at rush hour, flying through the streaming avalanche of cars, but sitting alone in the dark theater long after the credits had passed I realized that it was the son, it was the boy I had come back to see. In other parts of the film there were no real similarities, but when it was just his curls bobbing in the frame, just his small body covered by his mother's, the kid actor looked for all the world like Martín.

That night, I came home to find Gary spilled from his wheelchair, lying spread out across the kitchen floor. The kitchen was tiny, so his arms and legs were bent where they pushed against the walls and cabinets. He was snoring loudly. There was an empty bottle in one of his hands, and another beside his head, its wet lip just an inch or so from his open mouth.

At that moment, more than any time before, I wanted to follow his directions, to turn and walk from the trailer. No good-byes. I wanted to get on my bike and ride, even if the Schwinn would only carry me so far. I didn't think I could wait for however long it would take to make enough money; I didn't think I could spend another day there, with Gary, with Martín's parents knocking door-to-door, with his grandmother walking between the trailers at night, calling his name.

In my room, I counted the money from my mattress, knowing it wasn't enough, but hoping that it could get me part of the way, out of the city at least, starting along one of those routes from the map I'd memorized, those multicolored lines I saw every time I closed my eyes.

Ellie, I heard my father call. Ellie, I need you.

I couldn't do it. I couldn't leave. Maybe if he had been violent, or abusive, but he was just sick. He was just sad and trapped. How could I leave? I stuffed the money back into my mattress and returned to the kitchen. I pulled him into his chair, got him his pills, his bottle. His hair was wet with sweat, plastered across his forehead. He needed a shave and a bath. His smell filled the small room. I stood against the wall by the window and he drank and stared at me. It was like the moment after a fight, like the fights I used to have with girls at school, when the girl and I were completely worn out but still circling each other, wondering what was left, where we went from there.

Mid-June became late-June. It felt like rain, but not a single drop fell. The city was suffused with a steamy sepia haze, hot and oppressively humid. I stopped looking for bikes, and spent all my time looking for Martín. Everywhere I rode, I thought that I saw him. The streets were full of brown, dark-haired boys. The Romeros continued their search. They walked the neighborhood and took the bus to other neighborhoods to walk the streets there. They visited the police precinct every afternoon. Sometimes patrol officers gave them a ride home in one of the squad cars.

At the window, watching, my father said, "A kid missing this long isn't missing anymore. He's just gone."

The rumors continued cycling—two sisters or lesbians with handfuls of Jolly Ranchers in a yellow van—but they were becoming legend rather than news, stories I heard kids telling at the flagpole when it was getting late, to scare one another for the walk home.

Other grandmothers came to the park to watch the younger kids. Martín's grandmother was never part of them. It was like she was cursed, like her misfortune might be contagious.

I looked for Martín, and when I got burned out from that, when every kid I saw looked like him and I started to think it was pointless, I went to see the movie. I sat through the first hour and a half, fidgety, impatient to get to that late sequence, the race through the corridors. Alone in the dark, the woman's panic felt like my own, and I'd grip the arms of my seat and breathe with her, running through those endlessly branching corridors, trying to outrace the flood, until the boy's head appeared, and then we'd both grab him and sprint for the light, the sand. The water rushed over us, and I could feel it, the roaring *whoosh* overhead and then the small body beneath mine, Martín held safe in my arms.

The movie began to disappear. I had to ride farther to see it, out to Sherman Oaks or down to Westchester, by the airport. Usually, I was the only person in the audience. This was true during weekday matinees, but also on Friday and Saturday nights, during stretches of heat that should have driven people into the theater just for the air-conditioned darkness. At a theater in Redondo Beach, the old man in the ticket booth didn't even bother to charge me, letting me pass with a dismissive wave of his hand.

I was on my way to a theater in West Hollywood, crossing the intersection of La Brea and Sunset, when I saw the van.

It seemed like something out of a dream, some kind of mythical creature alive now in the bright afternoon of the real world. The van was yellow and rusty, with two women in the front seats. I could hardly believe it, but when they passed, I followed, climbing La Brea north. The traffic was getting heavier as rush hour approached, and I squeezed between lanes, my elbows and knees skimming the doors and mirrors of the cars parked along the edge of the street.

The van cut east and then north again on Highland, climbing through the canyon, past the Hollywood Bowl and along the raised freeway of speeding cars. Hoods and windshields slapped reflected sunlight into my eyes. The climb was tough, unrelentingly uphill. Sweat ran down my calves and forearms, making it hard to keep my hands on my grips, but I knew the crest would come soon. By the time I reached it I had almost lost sight of the van, but on the downhill drop I tucked into the frame of the Schwinn and lowered my head and let gravity pull. I flew down the hill, passing cars and pickups and tractor trailers, all rattling dangerously close from the speed. The wind rushed against my face, almost forcing my eyes shut. The bike shook beneath me, and for a moment I could imagine it bursting apart, frame cracking, tires bouncing, my body hitting the asphalt and tumbling, skidding, sliding, but it all held together, and I remembered what Donald always said when I brought him a Schwinn; *Not much to look at, but sturdy as a sonofabitch.*

Finally, the valley flattened out, and the van slowed, turning north again on Vineland. I knew that I needed to stay back, a couple of car lengths at least, so the women wouldn't notice me following. They continued up to where the freeway cut across the valley floor and for a second I worried that they were going to jump on, but at the next light they turned west, sticking to the surface streets, heading into Van Nuys.

I had no idea what I would do when the van finally stopped. I could imagine the women turning into one of the long gravel driveways lining each side of the street, coming around to the back of the van and opening the rusty-edged barn doors, reaching in to pull Martín out. They'd lead him back, squinting in the sunlight, toward one of the long, low ranch-style houses at the end of each of the driveways. And then what?

The van slowed and signaled, its right directional bulb blinking white behind the cracked plastic lens. I pulled to the curb and let the van continue along for a few houses. At the lip of a wide driveway, it came to a stop. A chain-link gate barred the entrance. The passenger door opened and one of the women hopped down and out. She was tall and lean, wore a western-style shirt checkered orange and blue. Her full helmet of dark hair was shot through on the sides with zigzaggy streaks of gray. Pulling a key ring from the pocket of her jeans, she unfastened the padlock on the gate. She swung one side open and the van passed through, and she followed behind, closing and locking the gate behind her. I could hear her boots on the gravel as she disappeared behind the high wall of hedges that divided their property from the neighbors'.

I sat on my bike, one foot on the curb, my heart pounding an elevated drumbeat. I was a good fifteen miles from home, from the Romeros. We had passed a gas station a few long blocks back; there might be a pay phone there, but I knew I couldn't leave the van. I began to pedal again, slowly. When I reached the gate, I continued cruising, looking up the long length of the driveway. The van was parked at the far end, both barn doors open. The interior was a black mouth, lightless, impenetrable. More high, ragged hedges lined the side of the drive, hiding whatever house was back there. The woman appeared again from around the hedge and leaned into the back of the van. It looked like she was speaking, like she was talking to someone, trying to coax them out of the darkness. Then another hedge reared up as I passed the property line, cutting off my view.

Waiting for a break in traffic, I crossed the wide boulevard, then turned back toward the direction from which we'd come. Far off to the south, through the mustard-yellow smog, I could see the tops of the hills we'd crossed a half hour or so before. I rolled back along the opposite shoulder, stopping again when I was directly across from the driveway. Through the passing cars, I could see that the woman was still leaning into the darkness of the van's hull, though now I was too far away to hear her voice. She reached in, stretching, trying to maneuver something out. I didn't know what I would do when I saw Martín. Flag down a passing car, maybe. Start screaming, waving my arms. Something, anything to draw attention, to get help.

She began backing out, pulling something along with her. It was like the van was giving birth, like those movies we'd seen in biology class, a farmer pulling a calf from a cow. For a moment I had an awful vision, the van disgorging blood, bone, meat. I pushed the thought away, refocused on what I would do when I finally saw Martín. I knew that I'd just have to ride straight over, climb the fence and run to him. There was no other choice. I wasn't going to lose him this time.

The woman stepped down out of the van, still pulling, and I saw then that she wasn't pulling a child, she wasn't pulling Martín. She was pulling a tire. She was pulling a bike.

The woman stood, holding it by the top tube. I recognized the body immediately, the tight angles, the slight downward bend of the handlebars, the bike's almost prayerful pose. It was a Colnago Super, Saronni red, blood red, with cream and tan accents along the grips and rims. I'd never seen one in person, only in magazines or posters on bike shop walls. It was the fastest thing going. Luigi Arienti had won an Olympic gold medal on a Colnago. Eddie Merckx had broken the world's one-hour speed record on one just a few years before.

The second woman climbed down from the back of the van, still holding the Colnago's handlebars. She was short-legged and chubby, seemingly a direct counterpoint to her friend or girlfriend or sister. They set the Colnago down carefully. The tall one held the bike upright while the short one slammed the van doors. The sound shot out across the boulevard, jolting me back.

The tall woman opened a padlock on the garage door and then pulled the door up and over. Together they wheeled the Colnago into the garage, disappearing inside. A few moments later they reemerged, without the bike, and pulled the door down again, snapping the padlock into place.

I didn't know what to do. I was filled with this incredible

anger. The women didn't have Martín, and that made me hate them even more than if they'd had him. It was like he'd been taken all over again; he was doubly lost, pushed further into a dark corner somewhere, alone. I watched the women at their front gate. I wanted to take something from them, like they'd taken Martín from me, again.

I could imagine swinging myself onto the Colnago's seat, gripping its handlebars, bowing my body into position. I could imagine the feeling that would come, erasing the anger, the hollow ache of grief. That bike was fast, light, strong. It could take me along any of the routes on the map, as far as I was willing to go.

Somewhere in the back of my brain, the green light flashed.

The women stood in the driveway, shading their eyes and looking out to the boulevard, maybe to me on the far side. A girl on a bike. Traffic flashed by, breaking the connection. When I could see across again they were walking back into their house, pulling the door closed behind them.

It was getting darker, the slow dusk settling in. I stashed my Schwinn in a messy tangle of bushes, then thought better of it and pulled the bike loose again, propping it up against a mailbox at the side of the street. Left out like that, I knew someone would take it. That was the way things worked. And that felt right. Like if I failed to grab the Colnago, if I got caught or lost my nerve, I'd have no way back.

I waited for another break in traffic, then ran across the boulevard to the driveway gate. I popped the gate's lock with my bump key and squeezed inside. The driveway's gravel crunched beneath my sneakers. I waited, listening. I could hear the women's voices, muffled a little, coming from behind the house. Then a whiff of burning charcoal, a little plume of gray smoke rising over the roof. Barbecue night. I crossed the driveway, trying to stay light on my feet. I used the bump key to open the lock on the garage door, then I lifted it, slowly, just a foot or so, just high enough to roll under. When I was on the other side, I eased the door back down behind me.

The garage was dark except for a small window in the back letting in a little of the sunset. I stood and let my eyes adjust. The light from the window was red and gold and reflected all around me, little glints like fireflies, or cigarette lighter flickers. I didn't know what was happening. It felt like I was going crazy, losing my grip. I tried not to freak out, but to let my eyes finish adjusting, until I could see the space clearly.

My sense of smell settled before my vision. Leather and rubber and oil. I knew those scents. And then I could see, finally. The flickers and flashes settled into familiar shapes—shapes from posters and magazines, shapes from dreams.

The garage was full of bikes. They hung from hooks on the ceiling, stood in neat rows along the walls, balanced half-disassembled in shop stands. There must have been forty or fifty, every make and model imaginable. A forest of glinting steel.

The Colnago sat in the center, flipped up onto its handlebars and seat. I approached it slowly, reverently, as if I could spook it somehow, as if it might ride away on its own at my touch. Its frame was cool and smooth in my hand. I turned it back upright, swung my leg over the frame, set my feet onto the pedals. The bike was impossibly thin. It felt like sitting on the edge of something, like I could slide off at any moment, or that it would just disappear when I started pedaling. I traced my thumb along the embossed edges of the Colnago's symbol, the famous black club stamped into the side of the handlebar stem. The garage around me flared, brightened, sharpening to perfect clarity.

I heard a cough from outside, back behind the house. I could smell meat cooking, hamburgers, pot smoke. I rolled the Colnago to the garage door. I'd only have a second to lift the door and ride down the driveway and out the front gate before the noise called someone out. I took a breath and held it. I could feel my pulse in my ears, the same heavy thump I'd heard so many times in the theater, running along with the woman, trying to outpace the flood. There was another cough, closer this time. I heard the house's screen door open, its hinges screaming. I grabbed the garage door's handle and pulled. The hole opened in front of me and I could see the corridors from the movie, the open square of light beyond. I pedaled through. The bike tried to buck beneath but I held it tightly, knees and elbows in, forcing too much and then backing off, letting it carry me across the uneven gravel toward the gate.

I turned my head for a second, looking back, a mistake, almost losing my balance. I saw the women coming out their front door. I saw the walls of water rushing through the corridors, could hear the roar close in my ears.

"Hey," one of them called. Then the other shouted, "Hey! Stop!" But I didn't stop, I continued pedaling, down the driveway and through the open gate and into the middle of the boulevard, dodging cars, holding that breath until I had broken free.

I took a different route back, making quick turns, looking for the van behind me, thankful for the growing darkness. The Colnago was even faster than I'd imagined, light and nimble, but strong enough to push, and so I pushed, riding hard all the way back.

The park was quiet; the alleys between trailers empty. I set the Colnago around the back of the trailer and ran inside. Gary was beached in his lounger, a bottle in one hand, staring at the TV. The screen was dark; the set was off. Sometimes he slept with his eyes open.

In my room I pulled the money from my mattress. I shoved a few clothes into a backpack. I had enough cash to buy more along the way.

From the other side of the park I could hear Martín's grandmother, her voice high and faint, a ghost's voice calling him home.

In the mirror, I looked and tried to see her, my mother, but all I saw was him. I wanted to tear out of my body somehow, rip it off me, as if it were a shell I could escape. I looked at the scars on my arms, on my calves and thighs, and saw them for what they were. Little exits, little ways out. I knew that if I stayed here, with my father's slow death, with Martín's grandmother calling his name, that I would return to that sharp edge, I would need it, and that eventually it wouldn't be enough, and I would find bigger blades, make deeper marks.

I wrote a note for the nurse and set it on top of the TV in the living room. I stared at my father for a moment from the other side of the room, as I had so many times, wondering what would come next.

I walked over to him, sleeping heavily in his chair. His hair was absurdly dark, dry as straw between my fingers. No goodbyes. That had always been his command, his wish. But you don't always get what you want. That was one of his favorite songs. Don't, can't. The Tick-Tocks covered it on their only record.

I leaned down and kissed his clammy forehead. I touched his cheek and whispered goodbye.

Riding the Colnago, the world stayed bright for a long time, much longer than it ever had before. Colorful and new, fresh, strange. I followed the most central route I had seen on the map. But for the rest of that summer, riding east, it really felt like I was following the movie. When I'd see its title on a marquee, I'd stop for the night, paying a little extra to roll the Colnago into the theater with me. I always kept it close.

Fort Apache, Jonesboro, Louisville. The glow of riding the Colnago began to fade. The movie became harder to find, then disappeared completely. But by then I knew it by heart, and during long stretches of riding or at night in some dark motel room I'd replay that sequence, following every twist and turn of the corridors, chasing that moment of discovery and relief when the mother finally finds her son.

On the first Sunday in October, I reached New York. The city was so much bigger than I'd imagined, a new world almost, but quiet, too, so early in the morning. I was out of money, so I sold the Colnago to a man in Battery Park. By then, it was just another bike. When he left me with the cash I turned into the wind and saw the shock of water, the sea pressing right up to the city's edge. I'd gone from one body to another. I walked down to the shoreline. The sky was gray and rolling, restless with an approaching storm. I let the tide pull at my sneakers and then took them off and walked out to where the water reached my hips, to where the city disappeared and all I could see was ocean. I felt so lost and alone. I wanted to cut myself, feel the sharp edge pulling through my skin. I wanted to steal something. I wanted to trade this feeling for another, even for a moment, but there was nothing left to take.

I could see the boy, his hair in the frame, so I wrapped my arms around his chest and held his body close. I whispered his name again. The water swelled. I had never learned to swim; I had always been afraid of water, but there with him, I took a breath and lowered myself, holding him tight, feeling his face in my hair, the water rushing over us.

I imagined him in the back of a van, or alone in some dark corner. I imagined his face in the reflected light of the movie screen, his hand on my wrist, his nose in my hair, breathing in. I imagined him in my arms. The current was so strong. If I stayed there I'd be pulled farther, deeper. I started to lose my balance. I imagined the escape pod, ready to leave the dying planet. I didn't want to go alone, I didn't know how I could go alone, but my lungs were empty, the current was pulling. I held on as long as I could, until I no longer felt his breath, his warmth, and then I lifted myself out of the water and opened my arms and let him go.

Acknowledgments

Linda, Jim, and Jenn O'Connor; the Anderson and Krugman families; Martin Garcia and Susan Weber; Ben Leroy and Tyrus Books; Alison Callahan, Brita Lundberg, and everyone at Scout Press; Jim Ruland; Rachel Harper, Robin Lippincott, John Pipkin, Chad Broughman, and the students and faculty of the Spalding University MFA program; Dana Spector and Zac Simmons; Owen Shiflett and Zack Parker; Jack Boulware and Eddie Muller; Laura Cogan and Oscar Villalon at *ZYZZYVA*; Michelle Franke at *The Rattling Wall*; Dani Hedlund at *F(r)iction*; Louis Armand at *VLAK*; David Blum and Carly Hoffman at Kindle Singles; Andrew Holgate; Philip Gwyn Jones; Cedering Fox; and MyAnna Buring.

In memory of Stephen Blow and Kit Reed.

With love to Karen and Oscar. And for Yishai Seidman: editor, collaborator, and friend.